Untouchable

Shattered Safety Book 1

Maree Rose

Untouchable

by Maree Rose

Cover Art and Graphics by Book Dragon Designs

Blurb

**Not many people could say they survived a monster.
But Lexi could.**

She thought she was free and clear of the monster from her past. But when that monster suddenly reappears hunting her she finds herself being forced to place her trust in four complete strangers.

Colt, Rome, Gabe and Hunt are all ex-military and the best at what they do, but can they keep her safe? Can they protect her from a monster?

As if that isn't enough, Lexi is also grappling with the strong attraction she feels toward her new protectors. The instant pull she experiences toward them is both exhilarating and terrifying, and she struggles to make sense of it all amidst the chaos and danger that surrounds her.

Can she protect her heart at the same time they protect her body?

Foreword

Hello readers!

Thank you so much for picking up my debut book!

Please be aware that this duet is a reverse harem, meaning our leading lady Lexi will not have to choose between her men, because #whychoose.

There is explicit language and explicit sex scenes, including encounters with more than one of her men at the one time. This is absolutely an adult romance and is intended for readers 18+ due to the language and content. Please do not blame me for your increased water bills due to cold showers as you have been warned.

There are a few possible triggers that will come up over the course of the duet. There are mentions of past trauma, past attempts of murder, past child abuse, past abuse of lethal skill, these have impacted on characters within the story giving rise to PTSD. If any of these things are triggering for you please do not read this story.

There will be additional triggers and darker content for the next book but I will warn you about those in the foreword of that book.

Lastly, this book ends with you hanging off a pretty steep cliff, there will be a post in my readers group where you can shout at me and throw an appropriate GIF my way about how this one ends... until the next book comes out in a couple of months. Also do not blame me for any damaged kindles or phones.

Thank you and I hope that you enjoy Untouchable.

PS. Please mum DO NOT READ THIS BOOK!

*For all the smut loving ladies
who want to be called a
Good Girl...*

Prologue

No matter how nice the day or how bright the sunshine is, there are always parts of the world where the light doesn't reach. The shadows and dark always win out somewhere.

Lying on the ground in one of those dark places, all I wished for was just a little sunlight to come through. Just one more moment of feeling the sunshine on my skin. The soothing feel of it that's almost like a gentle caress. A sense of warmth that gradually spreads over your body.

Because at that moment I felt so very cold.

I had never before felt a cold quite like what I was feeling at that very moment.

It's amazing how much color gets leached out of the world when the shadows creep in. But I could still make out the color that coated my hands even in the shadows. Red. Not just any red. Blood red, because that is exactly what it was.

The pain that had initially radiated from my chest had disappeared, but so had most other feelings. Numbness was taking over my soul.

Damn, why could the sunshine not reappear just for a minute? I just wanted a little fucking sunshine right now. Was that so much to ask for?

Instead, the shadows were getting darker.

Was night coming quicker now?

I swear it had only been morning a moment ago.

Maybe I should just get some sleep? But it's so goddamn cold. It feels like ice against my skin.

There was something I needed to remember. Or was it someone? Someone I saw today. Or was it that I was meant to see them? My mind is so fuzzy.

I rack my mind trying to remember what I was meant to be doing today. I don't think I was meant to be sleeping. What was I doing? Oh, that's right, I was taking out the rubbish from the restaurant. I had the breakfast shift, not the dinner shift. Why was I still here with the night closing in?

Wait, why was there blood on my hands??

I tried to lift them to look at them again, but they suddenly weighed so much. When had my arms felt so heavy before? Maybe I will have a sleep after all. It was so very dark. Or are my eyes already closed?

I can't tell anymore.

Ok, sleep it is.

Chapter 1

Alexis

The rhythmic bass pulsated through my headphones, setting a perfect pace for my run in the park. I was trying a new playlist, and it felt just right as I made my way along the circular footpath that wound through the sloping grassy hills and valleys of the park. It was all open air and sunshine, the few trees that littered the area were more central to the space and not close enough to the footpath to even create shadows where I was running. The air was fragrant with the scent of freshly bloomed flowers and the musky earth from the scattered flower beds throughout the space. The sun was bright and warm, caressing my skin as I ran and I savored the feeling of it.

As I jogged along the track, I passed by a few people scattered across the grassy areas. A young couple nestled under a shady tree, laughing and stealing kisses between bites of sandwiches, while in another area a family picnicked on a patch of sun covered grass, the children chasing each other around playing tag.

There was the occasional individual taking up other small blankets on the lush green grass, reading or eating. As well as a couple of guys playing some sort of ball game at the top of one hill, their muscles rippling in the sun and creating a distraction for any female with a heartbeat.

But no one paid me much attention as my feet slapped into the concrete. Even the other runners were easy to avoid, their attention focused with determination on their own circuits, as I made my way around the path for the twentieth time.

As I approached the end of the lap, movement drew my attention to a bench seat along the edge of the path. A man sat there watching me, his body tense and rigid. His hands were clasped tightly in front of him, and his elbows rested on his knees, which were splayed apart. His brown hair was neatly cropped on the sides but left a little longer on the top, allowing a stray wave of hair to fall across his forehead with the gentle breeze. A small frown twisted at his face and pulled down the corner of his lips as he watched me getting closer, causing harsh lines to appear in his otherwise very attractive face. My steps slowed upon seeing him waiting for me.

He was dressed casually enough. His dark denim jeans hugged his legs, while his practical, yet rugged, black boots looked like they had seen better days. He wore a simple black button-down shirt he had rolled up to his elbows to cut down on the heat of the day. As he shifted on the bench, reaching for the bottle of water he had rested at his side, it revealed the shining badge pinned to the belt at his waist next to the unmistakable holstered gun. Neither of those things surprised me, though.

My steps slowed to a walk as I approached, and I could feel my heart rate returning to normal and my breathing calming. I used my watch to press stop on the music playing in my ears. I extracted the earbuds and put them in the pocket of my gym shorts, raising an eyebrow at the water he offered me.

He huffed in annoyance when I didn't take the water from him. "It's sealed and unopened, you can check." He said, his voice deep and gruff as he waved it at me again, urging me to take it.

After another moment of hesitation, I accepted the water from him, and listened to the crisp crack of the plastic as I turned the lid to open it. As I took a few sips of the cool water, I watched as his frown deepened further.

"I thought you were meant to be taking it easy?" He said, his voice laced with concern.

I rolled my eyes at him and gave a slight shrug. "It's been almost two years. The doctor cleared me a long time ago to exercise and workout like anyone else now."

His deep brown eyes flashed with annoyance as he watched me take more tiny sips of water, and his lips pressed into a thin line. "I don't think he would have meant running at the speed you did for the last hour."

He obviously didn't know I'd actually been here for twice that long. I was confident he wasn't in this seat on my last circuit, so he must have been observing me from a different location. I had an urge to call him a stalker, but I decided against it.

I recapped the bottle to restrain myself and channel my frustration into something other than the thought of dousing

him in the remaining water to cool his temper. Or maybe I
should have taken that approach with myself. As much as he
deserved it, I knew it wouldn't help the current situation. I
could feel heat crawling up my neck that had nothing at all to
do with the sun that shone down on us. My brows drew down
as I felt my temper start to show on my face and I returned
his scowl.

"Why do you care anymore anyway, Kacey? You lost the
right to have a say seven months ago when you decided you
couldn't protect me and sleep with me at the same time."

A flicker of something unreadable crossed his face at the
same time a small frustrated growl escaped him as he looked
away from me to look towards the families and couples pic-
nicking on the grass. I could see him struggle to rein his own
temper in. His temper had always been like fire, but never
before quite like today. I studied him for a moment, watching
his face struggle with whatever internal battle he seemed to
have raged on.

I let out a deep sigh. The rush of air escaped me as I shook
my head. "What are you doing here, Kacey? I thought you
guys were done with me now." My gaze remained fixed on
him, waiting for an answer as I observed his face.

He flinched as he looked back at me. A flash of regret
crossed his face before he pulled his professional mask back
over his features as he rose from the bench. I should have
taken that as the warning it was, but of course, after two
years, I had obviously already become complacent again.

"Dominick has escaped."

My stomach instantly plummeted and a small wave of
dizziness swept through me. I immediately started quickly

going through my list of coping mechanisms in my mind. Focus. What sounds were around me? What could I feel? What could I smell? What could I touch?

My fingers squeezed into the bottle in my hand, the crisp crinkle sound of the plastic helping to focus me. The breeze rustled the leaves along the path at my feet. The cool condensation slid from the bottle and across my fingers. The familiar musk scent of Kacey's cologne filled my nose as he took a small step closer to me, jerking me from my inner thoughts.

"I'll go grab my go bag." I quickly turned away from him with the intention of heading straight to my apartment. I almost walked directly into the wall of solid muscle standing directly behind me that seemed to materialize out of thin air. I couldn't help the startled gasp of air at not realizing someone was that close to me and I hadn't noticed. It definitely did not have anything to do with him looking like a god in the flesh. Nope, not at all...

"I wouldn't do that if I were you." His voice was deep and smooth. It had a gravelly texture to it that affected me more than it should have.

I stepped back and let my eyes quickly roam over his impressive appearance, my mind instantly screaming military. And fuck me, did he make it look good. This man was power personified; it seemed to emanate from him. His heavily muscled legs were wrapped in black tactical pants and a tight shirt stretched across his broad chest, threatening to tear at the seams if he moved the wrong way, highlighting his muscular arms. There was a firearm discreetly tucked into a holster under his arm and I could make out the telltale sign of another at his ankle. Not counting whatever else he may have hidden in his tactical pants

Jesus Christ. Had I passed out or something from my run? He cannot be real, right? This whole situation could not be real.

I forced myself to tear my gaze away from the newcomer's impressive muscles just in time to catch the subtle twitch at the corner of his lips as he stifled a chuckle at my expense. Embarrassment heated up my neck, knowing I'd been caught checking him out, even if it was only for a moment. He had strong, chiseled features that led down to a defined jawline and sharp cheekbones. Aviator glasses shielded his eyes from view, but a whiff of sandalwood carried by the breeze told me he smelt as good as he looked. His hair was cut military-short on the sides and left spiky on top.

My brain finally re-engaged and gave me a metaphorical kick in the ass to try to get me moving. "I'm sorry, what? Why can't I do that?"

He huffed slightly. "Because, Princess, he was spotted outside your apartment. Your location has been compromised."

A chill slid along my spine as his words registered, but I guess my body had already done the panicking it needed to because all I felt at that moment was my temper flare. I looked quickly between the new guy and Kacey.

"Okay, for starters, who the fuck are you? And secondly, what the fuck Kacey?"

Kacey flinched again as I turned towards him, guilt written all over his face as he turned to make introductions. "Alexis, this is Colt, he's a friend. He and his team are going to take you to a safehouse." He looked down momentarily before confessing, the sound of regret clear in his voice. "Lexi, my office is the only one who knew you were here. We must have a mole. We can't trust my team anymore but you can trust Colt. He will keep you safe."

The concern and worry that shadowed his face was plain to see. I knew he was telling me the truth and it was hurting him that he was failing at something that was such an important part of who he was. I couldn't find it in myself to argue with him and found myself nodding slightly. "Ok," I breathed out, the stress of the last half hour started to bear down like a lead weight on my body.

He grunted and frowned at me, his brow scrunching up. "You're being a lot less hostile about this than I thought you would be."

Another fresh wave of dizziness hit me, my vision blurring slightly at the edges before refocusing again. I knew I was no longer panicking, maybe I did overdo it after all. I looked down trying to use the footpath to focus while I tightened my hand again on the cool water bottle in my hand.

The water bottle...

But that couldn't be right, I felt and heard the seal break. Kacey knew my paranoia about that sort of thing. I looked at it, trying and struggling to get my sluggish mind to concentrate on it. I saw what I failed to see by automatically trusting the seal on the bottle, a tiny hole in the plastic near the cap. I frowned and looked back up at Kacey.

"What did you do??" I could hear the slight slur in my voice as I pushed the words out, the struggle to focus became even more pronounced as my vision became hazy again.

"I'm so sorry Lexi, I hope you can forgive me, I didn't think you would be quite so accommodating for us. And I just need you safe."

My vision was going black and the bottle dropped from my partially numb fingers. I vaguely felt the strong arms that lifted me under my legs and back, my body then held against hard muscle.

And then all I knew was darkness.

I fucking hated darkness.

Chapter 2

Alexis

I would have liked to say that my return to consciousness was as slow and smooth as my descent into unconsciousness, but it wasn't. It was instantaneous. One moment there was vast nothingness, and the next my body had lurched straight up while I gasped for air.

I looked around me frantically to try to get my bearings, but my mind was taking nothing in. I could tell that I was in a moving vehicle, and my panic started to creep in further as my breathing became ragged.

Hands gently gripped my upper arm and shoulder from both sides of my body, and before I could panic further at the feel of them, a husky drawl came from my right. "Easy there, sweetheart, you're okay."

There is a slight southern accent to it, and for some reason it automatically cut through my panic like a calming blanket.

I took in deep gasping breaths and tried to calm myself. I was then able to take in my surroundings. Once again, I noted I was sitting in a moving vehicle.

A moving vehicle with four men. The vehicle was large because I still had a lot of breathing room around me. It had a crisp new car smell, but yet, the leather upholstery beneath me was soft, almost buttery against the back of my legs. I could hear the engine like the purr of a beast in contrast to the silence of the vehicle's occupants.

I was thankful that it still appeared to be daytime, and light was streaming through the windows. If it was dark, I was not sure my panic would have calmed at all.

I recognised Colt in the driver's seat, his attention focused on the road in front of him and his hands gripping the steering wheel while another guy sat in the front passenger seat, typing away rapidly on a laptop.

I couldn't really make out much of his profile from the angle I was sitting, except for the slight scruff along his jawline, thick black reading glasses and brown hair long enough to be tied at the back of his neck. A few loose strands fell forward to hang in front of his face as he concentrated on his computer.

I turned towards the direction the voice had come from, the man in that direction being the one holding onto my upper arm. I saw a lot of fair skin and a huge grin set in a face that almost made me swallow my tongue.

His features were almost verging on pretty but not quite. He had fine sharp angles, but definitely not delicate. His platinum blond hair was cut short at the sides but extra long on top, so long that the waves of his hair swept across his forehead to the side and almost reached his startling ice blue eyes. He radiated happy sunshine energy and instantly reminded me of a puppy.

A husky puppy.

The hand that was holding onto my other side fell away from me, drawing my attention to that side and my breath caught.

Well, hello, Mr. Hyde.

The name instantly popped into my head as I looked into a face that was a mirror to the happy husky puppy, but yet the complete opposite. His platinum hair was slicked back and the glint of metal at the corner of his lip drew my attention. The tip of his tongue flicked out against it before he turned to look out the window of the car again, dismissing me. There was an edge to him, like a sharp knife.

Colorful tattoos covered most of his exposed skin in deep and vibrant blues, purples, greens, and reds with a myriad of black lines creating shapes that I couldn't clearly identify at this distance. I instantly wanted to trace every single one.

With my tongue.

What the fuck was wrong with me?

I returned my attention back to the front of the car, looking out the window and seeing nothing familiar at all. We were on a long stretch of road with thick trees on either side blocking all the rest of the world out. I could feel Colt's attention moving between me and the road. I could tell he was waiting for me to panic, preparing to pull over if need be.

I took in a few deep breaths, my heart slowing back down again. Kacey obviously knew and trusted these men, and as much as Kacey frustrated me, I still trusted his judgment. I had to go with the logic that for the moment I was safe.

My throat felt like I swallowed sand. "Water?" I croaked out.

A clear bottle appeared in my eyeline from the happy puppy, and I eyed it briefly before meeting Colt's eye in the rear-view mirror. I knew I was the one to ask for the water, but I couldn't help being paranoid, Kacey had already proved my reason to be that way.

He gave a gruff chuckle. "If I wanted you to stay unconscious I wouldn't need to use the water, it's safe."

Comforting.

I took the bottle with a scratchy thanks and downed half the contents in one go.

"Easy, sweetheart, don't make yourself sick before you get to the safe house."

I relaxed back into the seat and took in the other occupants of the car again now that I was more clear minded. The happy puppy was still focused solely on me, and when my attention returned to him he flashed me another grin. "I'm Hunter, but you can call me Hunt."

Even his voice was cheerful.

"Lexi."

He chuckled and nodded at me. "Yeah, we know, sweetheart."

I felt the blush sweep across my cheeks, but he diverted my attention again.

"You already know Colton, the genius in the front is Roman, and my dark side over there is Gabriel. Like the angel."

My gaze flicked Gabriel in time to see him scratch his pierced eyebrow. With his tattooed middle finger. A not so subtle bird aimed directly at Hunt.

I couldn't stop the chuckle that escaped, and Gabriel's lip twitched in response. The whole vehicle seemed to relax at that, like everyone in it had let out a breath they had been holding.

His eyes slid back to mine. "You can call me Gabe."

Even his voice had an edge to it. But more gravelly, almost like he smoked frequently or had damaged his voice in some other way.

Now that I was not as much on edge, I took the time to take even more of my surroundings in and noticed that the guys sitting on either side of me didn't actually have that much on. They were both in black sweat shorts and tight fitting shirts. Gabe had on a lightweight jacket unzipped over his tight shirt with the arms pulled up to his elbows. I could see the edges of his colorful tattoos creeping up his neck, and when I concentrated on them I could see that they were flames. Their legs were muscular and being kept carefully at a slight distance away from mine to give me some semblance of my own space. Gabe's legs were all tattooed while Hunt was all clear skin.

A memory slid into my mind as I looked between them, my eyes widening as I looked back at Hunt. "You were in the park."

His laugh was loud in response. I could see it clearly again in my mind, the two guys playing ball in the center of the park were Hunt and Gabe. They had been there for almost an entire hour before I stopped to talk to Kacey. I had noticed them long before I had even noticed Kacey.

"Good to know you had at least a little awareness of your surroundings."

The snark from the driver's seat was next level as Colt sent a slight frown my way and my mind flashed back to the moment of almost walking into him because of not realizing he was standing behind me as I talked to Kacey.

I resisted the urge to stick my tongue out at him and let my head fall back against the seat with a huff as I looked at the roof of the vehicle.

"Okay, yes, I know I fucked up. I was distracted by Kacey. But can you really blame me? I would have thought I would be safe with a US Marshal standing right there."

Colt scoffed. "I think we can clearly establish that the US Marshals are no longer safe or to be trusted with your safety moving forward."

My head came back up at that and I looked at Colt with wide eyes. "Even Kacey?"

"Even Kacey."

His eyes flicked back to mine briefly and there was something in his gaze I couldn't readily identify, but in the next moment his eyes flicked away again and back to the road.

My frown deepened. "But I thought you and he were friends."

"We are. And that hasn't changed. But right now, you're our number one priority. And they are the ones that put you in danger." His eyes came back to me with a seriousness that almost stilled the breath in my lungs. "So no, we will not be trusting the US Marshals with your safety right now. And even on the very slim chance we did again in the future, you should always be aware of your surroundings at all times. No matter where you are or who you are with."

I mentally bit back on the *Yes, Sir* that automatically came to my mind at being reprimanded by Colt. I looked back down to my lap to disguise the blush that I could feel heating my cheeks. Colt's dominating personality was hitting me in a completely inappropriate way given the situation.

Trying to distract myself from my wandering thoughts, I tried to change the subject.

"So, this house you're taking me to, is there any chance it might have clothes that will fit me? I didn't exactly have the opportunity to pack."

"Our safe houses are fitted out for all situations and scenarios, so yes, there will be women's clothes there that will fit you."

I looked up wide-eyed at the husky new voice, only to meet eyes that looked almost like gold. Calling them brown eyes would have been a disservice. They weren't a deep dark brown like normal but reminded me more of liquid copper.

Roman had finally closed his laptop and was now looking at me over his shoulder. It was the first time I had really seen the last member of this team and he had no less of an effect on me than the others did.

All four of them were unfairly attractive. And I was about to be locked up in a house with them.

I was so fucked. And not in a fun way.

Chapter 3

Rome

To say I was concerned would probably be an understatement. We had only just finished our last job when Colt had received the call from Kacey about cashing in a favor that was owed.

The favor that was now awake and staring into my eyes with an intensity I hadn't felt before. It was my first time looking at her since she had woken up and I had to stifle my immediate reaction to her.

Her long brown hair was pulled up into a high ponytail, with a few strands escaping from the elastic band as a result of being carried and loaded into the car.

And her eyes, they were unlike any eyes I had ever seen before. They were hazel, but they were so vibrant that you could clearly see the distinct transition from brown near her iris to a vibrant emerald green at the outer edges. Her lashes were long and thick, creating a dark halo and making her eyes even more entrancing.

Despite the scent of the car, I could detect her floral scent. Roses, like the ones I grew up smelling in my grandmother's garden.

Her running outfit revealed a lot of smooth tan skin around her chest and shoulders and I could see some of the scars that marred her otherwise flawless skin peeking out around the edges of the material.

But I knew there was more hidden beneath the sports bra and tank she was wearing as I had only just then been looking at the raw and messy medical records and police reports on my computer.

I needed to pull my attention away from her again.

I could see Colt flicking looks at me out of the corner of his eyes while he split his attention between me and the last stretch of road through the thick trees to the safe house. I could almost see the many questions he had on the tip of his tongue, but I knew he wouldn't voice most of them until the appropriate moment.

I focused on the road in front of us and away from the beauty in the back seat. I could only just make out the concealed driveway of the safe house ahead of us, the slight change to the tree line that if you didn't already know it was there, you would miss until you had already passed it.

"Are we good?" Colt's gruff question was of no surprise and it was almost routine after the many times we had done this in similar situations.

"Yes, we're all clear." I responded quietly.

I had spent the entire several hour drive to the safe house erasing any evidence that Alexis or our team had even been anywhere near the location we picked her up from. On top of that, I also made sure that no evidence of our movements and travel could be found anywhere including looping or scrubbing clean any traffic cameras that may have potentially caught the movement of the vehicle we were in as soon as we passed them.

Then I had done a deep dive on the situation we now found ourselves in. Yes, the word concerned didn't quite cover it.

But those are conversations we needed to have in private.

As we got closer to the driveway I used the secure application on my phone to open the gate for us to drive through. The gate was almost a metal monstrosity of solid black painted steel and technology that if you didn't have access to get past it could kill you the moment you touched it. Once we were through the open gate I closed it again and fortified it before we started making our way down the long hidden driveway.

The trees formed a natural archway over the driveway, creating the illusion of a tunnel before revealing the two-story house. The house was painted in earthy tones of dark green and brown, blending seamlessly with the surrounding landscape and evading any potential aerial surveillance. I knew that even the pool, located at the back of the house, was concealed from view by a dark green roof.

At first glance, the house appeared unremarkable with its dark brown paneled walls, black window trims and doors, and deep green roof. But then it had been bought not to stand out at all.

It had been one of the houses we had bought some time ago, but was regularly maintained by trusted and vetted contacts due to its location, security, and size. It was perfect for what could potentially be a long stay given the circumstances and we knew we could have those same contacts deliver any necessary supplies. Plus there was a local woman we could trust to do regular housekeeping tasks.

The whole property had been bought through multiple dummy corporations to a point where it would take a very good hacker to untangle the web and by the time they got that far we would already know the location had been compromised.

As I pressed the button to open the garage door, Colt maneuvered the car into the double garage, gliding into the available space as if he had done it a thousand times before. I closed the door behind us once we had come to a complete stop, enveloping us in relative silence. After turning off the engine, Colt turned around to look at Alexis once again, his expression unreadable in the dimly lit garage.

"Hunt will take you in and show you where everything is. We will be in shortly. I do want to talk to you, but I will let you settle in first. Just come find me when you're ready," he said.

She nodded in response as Hunt slipped out the side door, holding a hand back to help her out of the vehicle. She looked one last time at Colt. "I'm sorry I haven't said it already, but thank you for helping me."

She didn't wait for a response, taking Hunt's hand and slipping out, closing the door softly behind her and following him as he took her inside.

Colt removed his sunglasses and hooked them over his shirt before raising a concerned brow in my direction. "What is it? I know what that look means. I'm not going to like this am I?"

We had been working together for far too long if he could read me like that.

I reopened my laptop and after logging back in I spun it in his direction showing him the information that I had found on Alexis. "The man she is hiding from? Her ex? Is Dominick Rossi."

Colt grunted like he had taken a punch to the gut. "Fuck."

Yeah 'fuck' was a good description. I didn't really think it quite covered it though.

The man was one of the worst. Somewhere between organized crime and street gang, Dominick Rossi had been the boss with a reputation for brutality and pain. Until someone had turned and given witness accounts that sent him to maximum lockup for life. That someone was Alexis.

I furrowed my brow, aiming a frustrated look in Colt's direction. "Did Kacey not give you that information? What did he even tell you when he called?"

Gabe shifted in his seat and leaned forward, his arms rested lightly on the back of the front leather seats as he peered at the information displayed on my screen. As Colt deftly scrolled through the data, Gabe's eyes followed each line with intense focus, his brow furrowed in concentration. The glow from the screen illuminated his face, casting sharp shadows across his features and highlighting the angles of his cheekbones.

The frown on Colt's face deepened, the lines became even more pronounced. "No, he didn't. He rang and said he needed to call in his favor. That a woman's location had been compromised and he needed her taken to safety. He told me he thinks his team has a leak somewhere, meaning he couldn't take care of it himself. He briefly ran through some basics about her, but that was it."

Colt continued to scroll through the information and I heard the moment his breath caught. I saw his eyes widen letting me know he had reached the medical records.

"Holy shit. How is she still alive?"

I could hear the shock and disbelief in Gabe's voice, and I could completely understand it as it was the same question I was silently asking myself not too long ago. To save them the time and confusion of reading the medical jargon, I briefly summarized the information for them, my voice steady and not betraying the turmoil I felt inside about it.

"According to the records they had only been together for six months before she had witnessed some of his dirty deeds and criminal activity, including the murder of a city official. Up until that point she had been clueless of his true identity. When she tried to leave him and he found what she had seen, he decided to attack her in the alley behind her work while she took out the trash as was her routine. He stabbed her six times in her chest. Miraculously it missed everything vital with the exception of a lung. Fortunately, her boss had gone looking for her, and upon finding her in the alley he managed to get emergency services there in time to keep her alive and get her to a hospital for emergency surgery."

A choking sound came from Gabe as looked at me startled. "Six times?"

It took great effort but I swallowed down the growl that rose in my chest. "Yes, according to what she recounted in court at his hearing he said, and this is a direct quote, 'it was one for each month he wasted on her.'"

Gabe shook his head and diverted his attention towards the door leading inside. I knew his mind was preoccupied with her currently being given the grand tour of the house by his twin. It was best that she was in the company of the happiest and most cheerful of us while we discussed this darkness.

I looked back at a frowning Colt, and his thoughtful expression told me he reached the end of the reports. "What do we do now?"

He focused back on me. "Not too much we can do, our current priority is to keep her safe. See what you can find to try to help Kacey and the authorities without risking our position."

He opened the car door and stepped out, apparently done with our conversation. I knew my friend well enough to recognize avoidance as his natural response to certain topics. "Are we going to discuss the other matter?" I asked.

He glanced back at me, his face a carefully constructed mask. "Which matter would that be?" he asked, raising an eyebrow.

I gave him a pointed look, refusing to allow him to dismiss the topic so easily. "You know exactly what I'm talking about."

Gabe chimed in from behind me with a chuckle. "Ah, you mean the matter of her being smoking hot and not technically a job? Or how we all could tell how turned on she was by his little display of dominance back there?"

Colt slammed the car door shut with a loud thud, cutting off Gabe's laughter before he stalked off into the house. I was grateful that Gabe didn't continue with that line of conversation. There was really no need to mention that we were all aroused by her response in turn.

Chapter 4

Alexis

The house was beautiful, for a safe house.

Hunt had shown me around the bottom floor of the two-story house with a running commentary filled with humor, charm, and cheerfulness. There was a large dining and living room that was central to the space with a lot of high ceilings showing the upper level that I could see at the top of a central set of stairs. The living room was filled with all forms of entertainment from gaming consoles to movies, and even a bookshelf filled with books. Next was a very large kitchen that caused some slight kitchen envy, a small bathroom was hidden under the stairs, and a hallway then led to an office and a well equipped home gym. All the main areas of the house were decorated with polished woods and warm country tones that added to the homey feel of the place.

Best of all was the large windows allowing sun to flood the rooms with light and warmth.

The house smelled clean and inviting, and it was clear that it was regularly maintained. Even the kitchen was stocked with fresh foods, as if the house had been specifically prepared for their arrival. Despite its function as a safe house, the space was undeniably beautiful.

When I saw the gym, it brought back the memory of going for the run this morning, which felt like forever ago. Once I moved past the brief wash of anger at Kacey for drugging me, I remembered to ask Hunt about my phone and smartwatch that I had noticed were absent in the vehicle.

"We left them with Kacey, sweetheart. Sorry to cut you off from everything, but there is always the possibility of those channels being traced, and we certainly don't want to take any chances of anyone discovering our location."

Following that, he led me up the open stairs to the landing on the second floor where he pointed out each of the rooms they would be occupying before finally showing me to the room he said was mine for the duration of our stay. The room had its very own ensuite and a well stocked closet full of various clothes in different sizes. It also had a large window overlooking some trees and allowing more sunlight to stream into the room.

He left me with the instruction to use whatever I needed and to try to relax.

I took in a deep breath as I looked at the room around me. It was very obviously fitted out and decorated with both genders in mind, with a neutral and natural aesthetic that appealed to all. The closet even contained an impressive collection of men's and women's clothing in a variety of different sizes. As I perused the closet, I came across a range of bras and underwear and the mental image of these muscular men potentially shopping for lingerie amused me.

The walls boasted a gentle shade of light brown, serving as the perfect backdrop for the striking black wood and metal bedroom set. A black leather armchair nestled comfortably in the corner of the room, adding a touch of coziness to the space.

After I locked the main door, I selected some comfortable looking leggings and a loose shirt and locked myself into the bathroom.

I frowned and bit at my lip as I took in my reflection in the mirror under the bright overhead lights. It was a testament to the turmoil I was feeling on the inside. My hair was in a disarray after first my jog, and then being carried and sleeping in the vehicle. Color was high on my cheeks and I internally put that down to Hunt's company on top of everything else.

Sighing, I took my hair out of the ponytail it's in and threw it up in a loose bun before spending the next half an hour drowning my chaotic mind in a hot shower. The scent of the berry body wash and fruity hair products soon filled the air and I mentally wondered who stocked those items.

I didn't want to think about the reasons for currently being locked away in this house with its built in protection detail. The past was an ugly place and I did not want to voluntarily visit it.

I knew I wasn't the same person I was two years ago when I was left in an alley to die. But that still doesn't stop that scared little part of me from resurfacing knowing Nick was out there looking for me at that very moment.

After he had realized his attempt on my life had been unsuccessful, he had tried sending one of his lackeys to finish the job in the hospital, only to fail again and sentence his lackey to death by cop.

From there he went so deep underground it took the FBI just over a year to drag him back out into the light again, and another four months after that before he stood trial for all his sins. He had been sentenced and locked away almost 7 months ago, and since I was still living a life under a new name and identity I was clear and safe.

I guess my life wasn't made for that kind of luck.

Dragging my thoughts from the darkness and my body from the shower, I took advantage of the other toiletries on the vanity including a moisturizer that felt and smelled divine before pulling my selected clothes onto my body.

Moving out of the room again, I wandered down the stairs and looked around taking it all in again.

Out of every window was a view of trees as though the house was built deep into a forest. With the exception of a pool area visible through the window looking out of the back of the house the trees were closed tightly around the property. It wouldn't actually surprise me if they had set up some way to even make the house invisible from the sky.

My guess was Google Earth had nothing on this property.

The men were nowhere to be seen, but I could hear music and movement in various areas of the house. Following one source of music, and the rumble of my stomach, I made my way to the kitchen and saw the very surprising sight of a sinfully tattooed Gabe stirring something in one of the pans on the stove.

The smell of whatever he was cooking was divine and also torture for my hunger. I tried to remember the last time I ate, and realized that after sleeping in I had only had a protein bar that morning before going for my run.

I could see what looked like sandwiches being kept warm in the oven also and contemplated what I had to do in order to get one of them into my belly.

He must have sensed my movement because he glanced back towards me over his shoulder. His lips curved into a slight smile before he refocused on his task. "We thought you might be hungry," he said. "Grilled cheese sandwiches and tomato soup is almost ready. Is that okay with you?"

I nodded in agreement, but then remembered that he wasn't looking at me. "Yes, thank you. Is there anything I can do to help?" I asked.

He looked back at me, his eyes scanned me from head to toe before returning to my face. It was difficult to read his thoughts, but I was finding all of them, apart from Hunt, to be hard to read, and even then I wonder to myself if the personality that Hunt showed the world actually matched what was on the inside.

He nodded in response to my offer. "Sure. Would you mind grabbing the plates and bowls and setting them out on the dining table?" he asked, his attention divided between me and the pot of soup that he was stirring.

As I approached him, he gestured to an overhead cupboard with his free hand. I reached up to retrieve the plates, and as I did so, my shirt rode up slightly, revealing a strip of my stomach. I could feel his eyes on me, silently watching, and a blush crept up my neck and onto my cheeks.

I cursed my body's reaction to his gaze as I met his eyes for a moment before making my way to the dining table to lay out the plates. As I returned for the bowls, I took a deep breath, trying to steady myself.

When I walked back into the kitchen his attention was back on the food and I stopped trying to wish for the earth to open up and swallow me.

I retrieved the matching bowls from the same cupboard, aware of Gabe's watchful eyes on me. As I turned back towards the dining area, I suddenly realized that Colt had snuck up behind me again. I gasped, and Gabe chuckled at my reaction. It was the first time I had seen Colt without his sunglasses, and his piercing green eyes held me captive as he looked at me.

Colt stepped forward and effortlessly took the forgotten bowls from my hands. I was momentarily grateful I hadn't dropped them in surprise. His humor was evident in his gaze, and a half-smile tugged at his lips. "How about I take these for you, princess, and you have a seat at the table? The others should be there by now too."

I knew I had to stop having such a strong reaction to these men. All four of them were ridiculously attractive, and it was affecting me far more than it should have. The events of the day had completely thrown me off balance, and I needed to find my footing again before I did something foolish.

Hunt and Rome walked into the dining area as I made my way back towards the table, feeling a bit dazed. Hunt grinned at me and held out a chair, gesturing for me to take a seat. Mumbling my thanks, I gratefully sat down while they finished setting the table and helped Gabe bring in the large plate of sandwiches and saucepan of soup.

Hunt slid into the seat on my left, flashing me another grin, while Colt took the head of the table on my right. Roman took the seat opposite me, with Gabe sitting to his right. Once everyone was settled, Colt filled up one of the bowls halfway with soup, then placed it and a sandwich on a plate in front of me. He then moved to serve himself while the others took that as some sort of signal that they could also descend onto the food.

We ate the delicious food in relatively comfortable silence, although I did feel the weight of the unsaid pressing down on all of us as we emptied our plates and bowls. But from the look Colt sent everyone when we sat down, I could tell that whatever questions I had needed to wait until we were done eating.

Colt relaxed back in his chair once he'd finished with an arm resting on the backrest of it while the other tapped a rhythm on the table in front of him. His eyes were intense as they focused on me in an assessing way.

"We already know everything that happened to you, so I'm not going to ask you to repeat your story for posterity or any of that bullshit," he said, his words coming out somewhat abruptly.

My breath caught in my throat and I forced myself to focus on the table in front of me, willing myself to take a deep breath.

I focused on the steady tapping sound of his fingers on the table and vaguely wondered if he did it on purpose, predicting my reaction, and I realized he had also waited to continue speaking until he could see I was focused on him again.

"I only ask for the moment that you tell us if there is anything at all we need to know that won't be in any of the reports we found."

I was aware of myself shaking my head at him but my focus was still hazy. My mind was scrambling over thoughts of what they would have read.

He nodded as though that is what he expected. "Then for now, just try to relax," he said, looking around at the others who began clearing everything off the table. "Get some sleep and don't think about what's happened. I understand that it's been a stressful day for you, and there will be plenty of time for questions and conversations later."

I started to offer to help with the clearing up, but Colt shook his head at me.

"Go and rest," he said firmly. "We'll all be around if you need us, but for now, just try to give yourself today."

Feeling befuddled and still sitting alone at the table, I realized that he was right. Maybe it was time to give myself a break and let the events of the day settle before diving into any more conversations.

Chapter 5

Colt

I felt like there was going to be at least a few deaths at our hands in the near future.

Kacey, for starters, for thrusting that glorious torture in a brunette package at us.

Secondly, whoever it was on Kacey's team that sold her out.

And then lastly, that asshole Dominick for ever laying a hand on her.

After we finished the task of cleaning up the dinner dishes and ensuring that Lexi was securely settled in her room, I headed towards the designated office space. As I entered, I spotted Rome already seated in front of the desk, engrossed in his laptop. The screen was flashing rapidly, making it difficult for me to keep up with what he was doing.

The office was quite minimalistic, with a simple, yet sturdy, timber desk and luxurious leather chairs arranged behind and in front of it for maximum comfort. Apart from the laptop that Rome was using, there are no other devices on the desk. However, there was a large screen mounted on one of the walls, which I knew could display the feed from any of the security cameras installed throughout the property. The room had a fresh scent of pine, indicating that it had recently been cleaned, just like the rest of the house.

Closing the door behind me, I made my way to the chair opposite Rome, sinking into it with a sigh. As he noticed my presence, Rome's eyes flicked up from his screen, and he raised an eyebrow inquisitively, silently inquiring about my state of mind.

"Just contemplating murder." I responded to his silent question.

Rome snorted a laugh. "Three people instantly spring to mind."

I grinned briefly, "See, you get me."

We had been working as a team for a very long time, so at this point we knew each other very well. Almost too well in some instances.

He stopped typing and sat back in the chair looking thoughtful. "You know we can't kill Kacey."

I almost pouted at him but refrained. "Not even a little?"

He laughed at me again. "No, we have known him for far too long. I think we could get away with a little blood and pain though, so go with torture instead."

I chuckled in response and let my head fall back against my chair with another sigh.

He continued, ignoring my dramatic reaction. "The other names that I know you're thinking about? Well, I'm absolutely behind you on those. Especially after reading those reports and meeting her."

I raised my head up again to look at him. My thoughts were swirling around my head as I thought about everything that had happened since the phone call from Kacey. The quick planning and move, and then the instant reaction we all had to her.

"I'm not imagining this, am I? There's something between us." I voiced my concerns to Rome, who nodded in agreement. His eyes darted towards the door before he spoke, ensuring that our conversation remained private within the walls of the office.

"You're not imagining it," he confirmed. "We've never had an instantaneous reaction like this to anyone before. And despite the chaos surrounding us, you can see that she's equally drawn to us."

I acknowledged his observations with a slight nod, but my thoughts remained focused on how to navigate the situation. "I'm just not sure how to proceed," I confessed. "We may not have a traditional professional relationship, but it's essential to maintain some level of professionalism for all our sakes."

He barked out a laugh and I grimaced, already knowing what he was about to say. "I'd really like to see you try that one on Hunt and Gabe. Can I be there when you spout that professionalism bullshit to them?"

I rolled my eyes and gave him a look and he settled down again. I sighed, rubbing at my temples, I could already feel a headache trying to develop. "What we do, what we like, isn't exactly a normal everyday sort of arrangement."

He was still grinning at me, not being dissuaded at all. "We have had this discussion before Colt, it works for us. And so long as we are clear about everything upfront, it works for them too. It's not like we haven't done it before."

I scoffed. "And look how those turned out."

"Just proof they weren't the right ones." He shrugged as though it's no big deal and simply proved his point.

"And you think she could be the right one? After not even a full day of knowing her?"

"Perhaps." He tilted his head as he thought about it some more. "My suggestion, for what it's worth, let's just let it take its course and see where it goes naturally. Don't stop whatever happens out of some stupid guise of professionalism, Colt. I know you. You need to move out of your own way sometimes." He gave me another look. "Her protection is a separate issue and shouldn't be a reason to put any brakes on. We are safe here and I'm working on finding out what I can to resolve the Dominick situation."

I dipped my head, acknowledging that I'd take it on board, but then my eyes moved back to his laptop, changing topics. "Have you found anything yet?"

"Breadcrumbs." He said with a shrug, "But you know I'll find the bread it belongs to before long. They aren't as good as me." He flashed me a grin.

I snorted. "Careful, or we will need another safe house just for your ego."

"Seriously though, I've found some little threads here and there that I'm trying to follow down the lines to the sources to confirm my suspicions before giving that over to our upstanding brethren. It always comes down to the mighty dollar, they just never remember how easy that is to trace. There wasn't just one recipient though, so if I'm correct, then Kacey's team is more like a sprinkler than just a leak."

I winced but there wasn't much more to be done with that. "Good, keep pulling on those and see what you can find."

He hesitated before continuing. "There is another thing though that we may need to monitor."

I raised an eyebrow and mentally prepared myself for yet another clusterfuck as he reached forward to tap something on his laptop.

A voice filled the room from what I realized was a voicemail message.

"Hey babe! You missed our catch up today! What gives? I'm going to make the assumption that you found some super hot guy who had distracted you with super hot sex because seriously that is the only legitimately acceptable excuse. Call me cause I want all the details!"

Something tugged at my mind as I listened to the recording, some small familiarity about it that I couldn't place, but the thought then slid away.

I groaned and let my head fall back again, closing my eyes. This shit storm just seemed to be getting worse. "That might be a complication. Keep an eye on it. Could you trace the number that made the call?"

He shook his head. "No, they were using a burner phone also, so I'm assuming perhaps someone she met in the program."

"Okay, let me know if you find anything more. I don't want to reach out to Kacey at all unless absolutely necessary given what we know. Though I know he will probably want to check in at some point."

"She may get a bit bored here, do you think she will cope with that?" His raised eyebrow showed his own doubt.

I thought about that for a moment. "Sam will be dropping in every few days to clean and restock the food. She may appreciate that female company even if it's only very brief every few days."

He nodded and closed the laptop where it sat on the desk before he sat back and looked at me again. "I know Kacey said she had a basic knowledge of how to shoot but it might be best to use the time we have here to expand on that and teach her some self defense skills."

"It wouldn't hurt. I'm sure she would appreciate being able to hold her own in a fight if she needed to."

He flashed a grin. "How appreciative do you think she would be?"

I chuckled and shook my head at him again, pointing to the door. "Get your ass out of here."

His humor was clear to see as he picked up his laptop and started to leave and it made me happy. His emotions were set at serious so much of the time that these brief glimpses at another side of him were great.

"Send Gabe and Hunt in here." I said in parting.

He flicked two fingers over his shoulder in a salute to acknowledge the order before he opened the door and walked out.

It took only ten minutes before the twins came into the room, closing the door behind them and taking up the seats across from me. While Hunt leaned forward with his elbows resting on his knees and his hands clasped under his chin, Gabe was the complete opposite, slouching down in the chair with an arm thrown over the backrest and his feet tapped a rhythm against the base of the desk between us.

I gave him a disapproving look and the tapping instantly stopped but I could see him start to use his teeth to play with his lip piercing and one of his thumbs started to spin at the rings on that hand. The nervous energy radiated from him and I made a mental note to get him into the gym for a sparring session to get some of that out of his system.

"Kacey said that Alexis had some basic knowledge of how to shoot. Rome and I think it would be a good idea for our resident sharp shooter to expand on that knowledge. What are your thoughts?"

Gabe gave a slight smirk and slid a glance at Hunt who was deep in thought.

It didn't take Hunt long before he gave a nod. "I think it's a good idea. I can take her out the back and see where she is at skills-wise and go from there."

I dipped my head in acknowledgement. "Thank you."

A grin stretched across his face and I could see the mischievousness of it from here. I internally groaned, knowing this was going to just stir us all up like Hunt was prone to do.

"Actually, I'm looking forward to it now. Showing her how to properly hold a gun. Wrapping my arms around her rocking body to show her the correct technique."

I felt my dick twitch in response to his words. The little asshole.

I didn't let anything show on my face as I watched the grin on his face get even bigger since the little shit knew me too well and knew that he was just sticking a needle in. I nodded as though I agreed with him before I spoke.

"That's great. I'll let her settle in for a few days and then I'll start giving her some physical self-defense lessons."

They both laughed as I then let the serious look fall from my face and flashed a grin at them.

"Fine, you win." Hunt held out his palms in surrender.

We sobered after only a few moments. "Just give her a few days to become more comfortable and then go from there. Don't rush her and don't crowd her. Did Gabe or Rome fill you in on her history?"

The flash of rage that crossed his face told me my answer even before he nodded.

"Rome is working in the background to hopefully eliminate the threat to her. Let's see what we can teach her in the meantime and keep her safe."

They both nodded to me and knowing that's going to be the end of the conversation they moved to leave.

"Gabe?" I called out as they started towards the door. He stopped to look back at me over his shoulder. "Make sure we spend some time on the mats tomorrow."

He flashed me a grin before proceeding out the door. Seeing what had happened to Alexis at the hands of that sadistic asshole had us both wanting to beat the shit out of someone, so I guess beating the shit out of each other was going to have to suffice.

I sank back into the chair, my thoughts consumed by the stunning brunette who now shared the house with us. Was it foolish of me to entertain the idea that Rome might be correct? That she could feel the same way we all do towards her? The idea of her reciprocating our desire flickered in my mind, but I quickly pushed it aside, not wanting to set myself up for disappointment.

Chapter 6

Alexis

It had been months since I last woke up screaming, having worked hard to build mental walls through therapy to overcome the nightmares of darkness and pain. However, after the day I had, it was no surprise that I found myself waking up with someone's hands on my shoulders and a scream caught in my throat. The hands sent me into a moment of panic, but my focus gradually cleared as a now familiar fruity scent filled my senses.

"Shhhh, sweetheart it's all right, you're ok now, you're safe."

As I whimpered, I blinked up at Hunt's concerned face, feeling the soft rub of his hands down my arms. It took an effort to pull myself out of the nightmare that had held me captive. My body shook, drenched in sweat, but Hunt didn't seem to acknowledge it.

The sheets were tangled around my legs from the tossing and turning I must have done. I had left the closet light switched on, its radiance sufficient to brighten up the whole bedroom. Now the hallway light that someone had turned on was also contributing to the overall brightness of the room. I heard a slight movement from the hall and saw Colt standing in the doorway, his face showing concern.

"I'm sorry, I didn't mean to wake you," I stammered out an apology, my voice croaky. I coughed to clear my throat as Hunt reached for the glass of water on the nightstand.

"Don't ever apologize for the after effects of what he did to you."

Colt's words were sharp as they left his mouth, his concern etched on his face as his eyes checked me over like I might have somehow hurt myself.

It occurred to me at that moment that I went to bed in only a workout tank and underwear, and that my nipples were suddenly appreciating the attention and I silently cursed my own body. It was absolutely not the right time to have that sort of reaction.

The problem with that was that none of us were wearing much in the way of clothing with both Hunt and Colt only in loose gym type shorts and bare muscle.

Did I mention the bare chests? And muscles?

My face flushed with embarrassment, and I instinctively curled my legs up towards my chest in an attempt to conceal the effect their focused attention is having on me. However, my efforts proved futile as the movement of the sheet revealed a glimpse of my bare leg.

I saw Colts eyes momentarily flare with heat before he looked away and down the hall and the look was gone by the time he looked back at me. "It's still very early and you should try to get a few more hours of sleep."

Hunt held the water glass up for me again. "Do you need something to help you sleep?"

My mind automatically went to something not so medical even though I knew that's not what he meant but I quickly shut down that train of thought.

Stupid hot men with their stupid bare chests.

"No it's ok, I should be fine." I croaked.

Hunt gave me a look as though he didn't believe me. "Would you like one of us to stay here with you?"

Fuck, why did he have to go and reactivate that thought process again. Shutting that shit down again in my mind, I gave it a serious thought and remembered that having Kacey in bed with me did help in the past when I was still having nightmares.

I nodded slightly at Hunt, who then turned to Colt, and the latter responded with a brief nod of his own.

Hunt moved away from the bed and into the closet and returned only a moment later pulling on a shirt he must have gotten from the supplies there. He left the closet light on as though knowing I needed it and even though the hall light was also still on, I noticed that Colt had disappeared again and I assumed he had gone back to his own room.

Hunt lifted the sheet slightly and slid into the bed from the door side creating a barrier between me and the door. He laid down on his back and then reached over and dragged me against him, completely ignoring that I was a sweaty trembling mess, shifting us both around until he was happy and comfortable. Perhaps taking a few more liberties with me than would be normal. What that equated to was me clinging closely to his side with one of my legs over his and a hand cradled against his chest. An awfully intimate position for people who hadn't been intimate.

I felt his cock twitch against my leg and my face flushed with heat again.

"Ignore him sweetheart, it's automatic for him to want to say hello to the pretty girl pressed into my side." He gave a soft chuckle but his arm tightened around me just the same to keep me there. "Close your eyes and get some sleep."

My eyes obeyed him easily and as I took a deep breath, I noticed that his breathing had slowed down, and I could feel the gentle rhythm of it under my hand. It was a comforting feeling, one that lulled me back towards sleep.

Suddenly, there was a shift in the room, and I cracked my eyes open to see that Colt had returned. He was wearing a shirt now, and he moved over to the armchair in the corner of the room to get comfortable. It's then that I realized he's staying with me, and my eyes widened with surprise.

As he settled into the armchair, he caught me watching him. His voice was a soft rasp as he spoke, but it's enough to put me at ease. "Sleep," he said, and without hesitation, my eyes drifted shut once again. As I sank back into slumber, I could feel myself being pulled under quickly and effortlessly.

In the end, it didn't even take me twenty-four hours for the stress to get the better of me.

It was only mid-morning, but I'd already worn a path into the soft, tan-colored carpet in front of the TV in the lounge room. I'd spent the morning aimlessly wandering around the house, trying to distract myself.

Meanwhile, Colt was lounging on the plush, comfortable sofa, his nose buried in a book. He was doing his best to ignore my frazzled state, as if this were just another average day. Like his completely ignoring the fact that he was currently hiding an emotionally charged woman being hunted by a criminal was totally normal.

Okay, maybe I was feeling a little dramatic.

I glanced over at Colt once again, biting my thumb nail anxiously. My other arm was wrapped tightly around my body as I tried to manage my stress. "So what do we do now?" I asked him.

"We wait." he replied calmly, his eyes still fixed on his book. His calm demeanor was infuriating, and I felt a surge of anger rise within me. How can he be so relaxed at a time like this?

That managed to stop my pacing and I looked at him dumbfounded, was he serious? "That's it? That's your big plan? Wait?"

He flicked a quick glance in my direction, his eyes peering over the top of his book before returning to his reading with a sigh. "Chill, princess," he said in a calm, collected voice.

But his words only served to make me feel even more agitated. My eyes widened with disbelief as I shot him a withering look. "Chill? Are you kidding me? There is zero chill here!" I retorted, my voice rising in pitch and volume.

As I glanced around the room, my nerves felt like they're on edge. Every creak, every gust of wind made me jump, and I couldn't seem to shake the feeling of being constantly on edge. Maybe I was being a bit over-dramatic, but could you really blame me? We're hiding out from a dangerous criminal who was intent on finding us, and every moment felt like it could be our last.

He glanced up from his book once again, giving me a droll look. "Princess, our one and only job is to keep you safe and alive," he said with a hint of exasperation. "Finding and recapturing that asshole is in the hands of the US Marshals and the FBI." He gestured with his hand as though indicating an invisible team of agents.

I let out a bitter scoff in response. "Really? The same US Marshals who posted a big 'Here's Alexis, come kill her' sign?" I threw my hands up in frustration before resuming my pacing across the carpet. I was so anxious that I barely even noticed Colt getting out of his seat until he stepped into my path and put his hands firmly on my shoulders, stopping me in my tracks. The pressure of his fingers was comforting, and I found myself leaning into his touch.

His eyes were intense as he gazed into my panicked eyes. "Look, the only people who even know about this house are currently inside it or are absolutely loyal to us. Right now, nobody even knows you're with us. Rome erased any trace of our journey here completely, and Kacey even called me on a burner phone to get my help. You're safe here."

His words and reassuring touch had the desired effect, and I felt some of the stress and tension within me begin to release. My shoulders slumped as I took a deep breath, trying to calm my racing heart. For the first time since we arrived at this safehouse, I allowed myself to believe that maybe, just maybe, I might make it out of this alive.

He must have seen this on my face because he gave my shoulders another squeeze before softly sliding his hands away again. "You have a whole house at your disposal. A gym, a kitchen if that's your thing, books, and gaming consoles galore here. There is a lot of stuff to entertain you. I'll even put my book down and watch a movie with you if you want. Just don't go outside without one of us."

He flashed me a grin before ambling back over to sit on the couch and pick up his book again before I could even respond to the offer.

I let out a frustrated huff and placed my hands on my hips, hoping to convey my annoyance. As I watched him, I could see his eyes darting across the page, and I could hear the rustling of the paper as he turned it. He was completely absorbed in his book again. I waited for a moment but he just kept reading so I huffed again and turned to stomp away, ignoring his soft chuckle that followed after me.

I paused in the doorway, turning to face Colt once more. I fixed him with a curious gaze, my eyebrows furrowed slightly. "Why do you call me that?" I asked, my tone hinting at a mix of annoyance and genuine curiosity.

Colt set his book down on his chest and fixed his attention on me. His lips curled up into a half-smirk and his brow raised slightly, his eyes sparkling with amusement. "Call you what?" he replied innocently, though I could tell he was fully aware of what I was referring to.

I rolled my eyes, knowing full well that he was just playing with me. "'Princess'," I said, miming air quotes around the word.

Colt chuckled again, the sound deep and low. "Maybe I'll tell you one day," he teased, a playful glint in his eyes.

I felt a slight blush creeping up my cheeks as I realized how easily he could get under my skin. "But not today?" I asked with a hint of exasperation.

He grinned widely, his eyes sparkling mischievously. "Not today," he confirmed, before picking his book back up and returning his attention to the pages, effectively dismissing me once more.

Stupid men.

Stupid hot men.

Chapter 7

Alexis

S oon after the conversation with Colt, I made my way to the gym to release my pent-up frustration on the tread-mill. Without my phone, I was left with the sound system in the corner, which offered a variety of workout playlists. A pulsating beat filled the room, setting a good running pace for me.

The gym was impressive and had clearly been renovated with the intent of helping the men keep in shape during their stays. The equipment looked new and the room smelled freshly clean. Although there were no windows, the overhead lighting was thankfully bright and the air conditioning kicked in automatically upon my arrival, providing a cool and re-freshing atmosphere.

The walls were painted in a shade of gray on three sides, while the fourth wall was entirely covered in mirrors. I had to remind myself not to make any comments about vanity. My mind wandered as I ran, and the sound of my feet pounding against the treadmill mixed with the beats of the music.

I had believed that I had moved on from my past and was no longer afraid for my life, but that asshole Dominick had ruined everything once again.

Just thinking about him made the scars on my chest itch, as though they were reacting in sympathy.

Yes, I hadn't actually ventured out socially for years, and Kacey and I had broken up months ago, but I did have a best friend I spoke to and caught up with regularly.

As I ran, I remembered that I had missed a planned meet-up with my friend the day before and I almost stumbled on the treadmill at the realization, knowing that my friend would not take kindly to being stood up. I made a mental note to check if I could send her a message, but also considered that it might be safer for her to be unaware of my situation.

Fucking Dominick.

As I continued to run on the treadmill, my frustration and anxiety mounted, causing my pace to increase. The physical exertion of my body caused sweat to bead on my skin, starting between my shoulder blades and trickling downwards. I knew that I needed to redirect my thoughts before they consumed me and triggered a downward spiral. My therapist had taught me the importance of recognizing these negative patterns and breaking free from them, so I made a conscious effort to focus on positive thoughts instead.

As my feet continued to pound against the treadmill, my mind began to drift to the four men that have been occupying my thoughts recently. I find it strange how I've had an instant reaction to all of them, something I've never experienced before. With Kacey, it had taken time for our relationship to develop and even though it ended, I didn't feel all that surprised or upset. I knew I had been using him as a distraction from what I was going through at the time, but we still had a genuine friendship that remained after the sexual aspect ended.

I've had sexual relationships in the past and enjoyed them, but these men seemed to be on a whole other level. I couldn't quite explain the intensity of my attraction to them. It was like something primal had been triggered in me, drawing me to them even though I barely knew them.

I couldn't even really tell if they had any interest in me in return, or even if they liked me as a person. There was a nagging fear at the back of my mind that they might only see me as a job, a responsibility that they needed to take care of until Dominick was caught. The thought was disheartening, but it was not entirely unfounded. They had been hired to protect me after all, and it was possible that their attentiveness and concern for me was purely professional.

Fuck. Why did my life have to be such a mess?

As I started my cool down on the treadmill, I gradually reduced my pace to a brisk walk. Suddenly, a noise to my left caught my attention, and I was grateful that I had slowed down. Otherwise, I might have tripped and became a mess of injured limbs. And died from embarrassment.

Forget Dominick, these men were going to kill me simply by taking off their shirts.

Colt and Gabe had obviously not long ago come into the gym and made their way directly to the sparring mats, where they were now wrapping their hands with tape and stripping down to just their shorts.

Fuck. Me.

I felt my heart rate pick up again, and my cheeks flushed as I tried not to stare.

They had to be trying to kill me. Maybe they were some devious new torture sent from Dominick.

Colt glanced in my direction and made his way over to the sound system. Was I imagining the heat I saw flash in his eyes when he looked at me? That couldn't be right. Right?

"Can I change the music, princess?"

Was I drooling?

Shaking myself from my thoughts I nodded to him. "That's fine. I was finishing up anyway."

God, was my voice all breathy? I was absolutely blaming my intense workout for my sudden lack of composure. I hit the stop button on the treadmill, relieved that it hadn't short-circuited due to my drool.

Gabe smirked at me as I glanced his way. "You don't have to leave on our account," he remarked.

I sipped at the water I brought with me. "I'm not. I've been running for a couple of hours so it's time for a break."

Just to prove a point, I put the water back down and started stretching out my muscles as Colt moved back to the sparring mats after changing the music to something heavier, the vibrations of the bass filling the room.

As I bent down to stretch my legs, Gabe got a full view of my tight leggings-clad ass in the mirror behind me. I caught his reflection in time to see him bite his fist and I almost snickered.

Except Colt chose that moment to land a cheap shot at the back of Gabe's leg, taking full advantage of his distraction.

I ducked my head to hide the grin that spread across my face from ear to ear.

They started circling one another on the mats and I knew I needed to leave the gym. Before my drool became a real hazard, because damn. They were absolutely dangerous. To a female's libido.

As I walked through the spacious open areas of the living room towards the stairs, I caught sight of Rome sitting at the large wooden dining table, his fingers moving at lightning speed on the keyboard of his computer. Curiosity got the better of me, so I decided to detour and approach him, even though I was aware that I was likely still emanating the scent of sweat from my workout.

Rome had been the one that I interacted with the least, and I knew while I smelled of sweat probably wasn't the best time, but I figured it wouldn't hurt to simply touch base with him.

As I neared him, he stopped typing and looked up, his eyes scanning me in one swift glance.

"Hi." I said, feeling awkward, I figured an awkward wave would have fitted into the approach perfectly but I restrained myself from that further embarrassment.

"Hey, are you okay?" he asked, tilting his head and looking at me with such intensity that it felt like he could read my thoughts and emotions with just a single glance.

I nodded in response. "Yeah, I was just heading for a shower, but I saw you and wanted to check in."

He smiled and raised an eyebrow, causing a blush to spread across my cheeks as I averted my gaze.

"I wanted to check in and see how the search for Nick is progressing and if there's any news about getting him locked away again," I said, my voice laced with concern.

His smile quickly faded again and he regarded me with a serious expression that made my heart sink.

"I'm sorry, there hasn't been any progress yet. We're doing everything we can, and I promise you that he will be behind bars soon," he assured me, his voice full of sincerity.

I nodded, trying to push away the disappointment that washed over me. I knew that finding Nick was a difficult task, and it wasn't just our group who was on the hunt for him. But that knowledge didn't stop my need for assurance that I would no longer have to live in fear.

Rome's smile returned, attempting to lighten the mood. "Are you that eager to get rid of us?" he asked, clearly teasing.

My eyes widened in surprise before a protest formed on my lips, but he quickly raised his hand to stop me, his smile growing wider. "I'm just joking," he said, and I couldn't help but smile in response, even though I still didn't know how to read Rome.

As if to prove my point his face became serious again. "You look like you just spent hours running."

I nodded slowly, the change in conversation abrupt but still welcome. "Yeah, I just finished up since my legs had decided they had enough. I was just heading to a shower."

He nodded as though he approved of my plan. "Running can be good, but just be careful you don't overdo it. If you need a running partner, any one of us would be happy to join you."

The thoughtfulness warmed me as I mumbled my thanks before I started to walk towards the stairs again. But then I paused and turned back as my earlier thoughts came back to me. In the process I caught yet another one of them checking out my ass.

"Umm, what are the chances of getting a message to someone?"

He raised both eyebrows at me, totally unashamed at just getting caught checking me out. "Your friend you were meant to meet with?" he asked.

I froze, surprised that he knew about my plans with my friend. "How did you...?" I started to ask, but he cut me off.

"We are monitoring your phone, and she left you a message," he said matter-of-factly.

I felt a quick flash of temper. "And I'm just now hearing about it?"

He was laughing at me, not out loud but I could tell by that twitch at the edge of his lip that he was laughing at me on the inside. "And what would you have done about it if I had told you?" he asked.

I opened my mouth to tell him exactly what I would have done but I came to a stop. Well, fuck. I snapped my mouth closed again, grinding my teeth.

He nodded as though my silence was confirmation that he proved his point. "I am keeping an eye on it, if she calls again I will get Kacey to reach out to her. It's safer if we don't make direct contact right now."

Okay, I guess that was logical. Why did he have to go and be so logical? I nodded to him in acknowledgment. I did appreciate it.

I could still see a smile at the edge of his lips. His eyes were still watching me intensely, as though he could read my inner thoughts.

Rome's tone turned serious as he spoke. "On that same note, you will get very brief female contact every few days. There is a housekeeper that has been maintaining the house for us. She has been thoroughly vetted and is trustworthy, but please just be careful when speaking to her to not disclose anything about who you are or why you are here."

My mind raced with the idea of a woman being in close proximity to these men. It's a strange feeling, almost like jealousy or possessiveness, but I quickly dismissed those thoughts as irrational. After all, there was nothing between us, no romantic or even platonic connection that would warrant those feelings.

I nodded, acknowledging Rome's warning. It was a small reminder that despite the relative safety of this house, there were still risks and precautions to be taken.

I managed a tight smile, hoping it didn't look as forced as it felt. "I'm familiar with the drill, Witsec, remember?" I tried to keep my voice steady, but I could feel the anxiety creeping in.

He nodded in acknowledgement, and his smile was gentle.

"You should go have that shower before your body cools down too much. It will help your legs," he added, breaking me out of my thoughts. His words jolted me into action, and I realized that my body is still tense from the earlier run. I thanked him again, and hurried upstairs to the safety of my own shower.

Chapter 8

Alexis

The next few days passed in much the same way. Wash, rinse, and repeat.

With the exception of the arrival of Sam on the third day. I was introduced to Sam as Alexis by Rome, who informed her that I was their assistant and was there to help organize things for them while they took some time off. Rome later told me that Sam had access to visit every three days with laundry and food. They thought it would be beneficial for me to have a trustworthy female visitor, even if it wasn't constant.

Sam was a woman in her forties, with a head full of tight brown curls, warm brown eyes, and a face full of freckles. She had a maternal aura around her, and as she moved through the house, the scent of pine lingered in the air. She tutted under her breath as she cleaned up anything untidy, according to her standards, and collected the dirty clothes to take away and wash.

Sam was a cheerful and friendly person, just like Hunt, and she couldn't stop gushing about how pretty I was when we first met. I later cooed over the pictures she insisted on showing me of her little boy Nathan who appeared to be around six years old. We even sat and had coffee and a slice of cake together before she left again with a promise that she would bring something sweet on her next visit.

The nightmares still plagued me during the night and Hunt was always there to soothe me and help me back to sleep under Colt's watchful eyes.

By now I knew the routine of all the men in the house. In the mornings they would all go about their own tasks. Rome would be checking all the electronic security of the place while Hunt checked all the various weapons that I knew were stored around the house, it didn't matter that nothing had happened in the twenty four hours prior he would still check them all. Meanwhile Colt and Gabe did a full perimeter check, walking along the large security fence that wound its way around the property mostly hidden by the forest surrounding the house. It's what they did every morning without fail.

They took turns cooking meals and the rule was to sit down together for dinner, and anyone who was absent was hunted down before anyone started eating. It created a lot of laughter when Colt threatened to drag Gabe out of a shower.

And at each meal Colt dished out my food before anyone else was allowed to serve themselves. It was a very old fashioned gesture but still touched something deep inside me that I didn't want to look at just yet.

Colt had a preference for healthy foods, while Hunt loved pasta dishes. Gabe, on the other hand, preferred comfort foods like the grilled cheese and soup I had on my first night.

Rome balanced things out with stir-fries, which was a happy medium between healthy and tasty. It seemed like we were all settling into a routine.

It was easy to fall into a routine with them. They made it easy.

The evenings after dinner would find us all in the lounge room where we would either watch a movie or play one of the many gaming consoles lined up on the entertainment unit. I had been handed so many gaming remotes and had crashed so many strange-looking cars that I had lost count. Despite my lack of skill, they never made me feel out of place, and the good-natured teasing only helped me to feel more comfortable and like I had been a part of their group for years.

No one ever commented about my need to turn all the lights on in the house the moment darkness started to creep in, they even started to do it for me without a second thought.

The banter between the men was next level, and I had noticed that quite a few of these interactions came with wagers for household chores or other not-so-chore-like tasks. For example, I witnessed the ever-controlled Rome perform an almost full strip tease because he came last in a very intense round of a car racing game before he put his foot down on going any further than his black boxer briefs. As he turned to retrieve his shirt from where he threw it, I caught sight of the stunning full-length tattoo of a fallen angel on his back. The feathers and wings spanned all the way across his shoulder blades and started tipping down his arms. I was so distracted by the sight that I almost had to fan myself and I then missed the full view of his brief clad ass as he bent over to retrieve the material.

Hunt, always the joker, was quick to snicker at me and use his finger under my chin to close my mouth. I responded by giving him a punch to the arm that he pretended actually hurt when I knew it probably only felt like a mosquito.

It was clear that they all enjoyed spending time together, and the relaxed atmosphere made it easy to forget the dangers that were still lurking outside.

I never broached any deeper topics with any of them, choosing to wait a little while before I start interrogating them to get to know them beyond the surface level.

If you didn't know any better you would never have been able to tell that I was currently hiding away from a mad man trying to stay alive.

As I walked down the stairs on the fourth day after we arrived at the safe house, my ears were caught by the beats of a song coming from the kitchen. The rhythm was so familiar that I couldn't help but follow the sound, deviating from my intended destination towards the living room. It reminded me of the playlist I had enjoyed in the gym sound system.

As I stepped into the kitchen, I was surprised to find Hunt with his back facing me, his hips swaying in time with the music. He was wearing slim track pants that clung to his legs and a tight shirt that accentuated his toned muscles leaving little to the imagination. The sun shining in from the window made his platinum hair glow like a halo around his head.

I must have made a noise or caught his attention, as he turned around to face me, flashing me a grin that's both charming and mischievous. "Hey," he greeted me warmly, his voice laced with his usual brightness.

A smile tugged at the corner of my mouth as I returned the greeting. "Hey." The way his eyes sparkled and the playfulness in his demeanor were contagious, and I couldn't help but feel more at ease in his company.

Hunt's eyes scanned me up and down, taking in my appearance. "How are you doing, sweetheart?" he asked, his voice soft and gentle.

"I'm good," I replied, a small smile tugging at the corners of my lips. "I was just on my way to watch a movie, but I heard the music." I thought about it for a moment. "Would you like to watch a movie with me?"

He chuckled and looked back down at what he was stirring before looking back at me with another grin. "How about I make you a deal? If you help me with these cookies, I will watch a movie with you."

I considered his offer for a moment, tapping my finger against my chin. "Hmm, I'm not sure that's a fair trade," I said teasingly.

He pointed the spoon at me, a mischievous twinkle in his eye. "I'll even let you put on a chick flick. And I won't complain once."

I laughed, the sound light and carefree. "Okay, deal."

As I moved closer to the counter, I noticed the array of ingredients lined up in a neat row, ready to be mixed together. Hunt started to explain the process of making cookies as we worked together, his hands moving quickly and expertly. The kitchen was filled with the sweet smell of sugar and flour, and the music that drew me in still played in the background.

Our movements soon fell into a comfortable rhythm as we mixed and stirred, occasionally breaking out into a dance move or two. The beat of the music seemed to guide our actions, and soon we're both laughing and smiling as we work.

I stole a glance at Hunt and noticed his lean, muscular frame moving fluidly to the music. He caught my gaze and flashed me a grin that made my heart skip a beat.

Suddenly, my curiosity got the best of me and I decided to ask him how old he was. He didn't seem to mind and chuckled as he continued to work on the dough.

"I'm 28," he said. "And Gabe is too, as you might be able to guess."

I nodded, realizing that they're only a couple of years older than me. Something I'm sure he already knew.

"And before your curious mind asks, Rome is about to turn 30 next month," he adds, "and Colt is 32."

As we started to spoon out the cookie mixture onto the baking sheets, I could feel the smooth texture of the dough between my fingers. We used our hands to roll them into perfect balls, carefully placing them onto the tray.

I bumped my hip playfully against him, causing him to pretend to stumble. "And I'm assuming that protecting women from killers isn't your everyday job," I teased.

He laughed heartily. "You'd be surprised," he replied, flashing me another charming grin. "We pretty much do what we're paid to do, within reason. Diplomats need bodyguards, they call us. A hostile situation requires more skills than the average uniform can provide, they call us. An enemy is entrenched somewhere that our authorities can't get to, they call us. Think of us as special jacks of all trades."

As he explained, my mind started racing at a million miles an hour. "So someone is paying you to keep me safe?" I asked, coming to a sudden stop.

He stopped moving and turned to face me with a serious expression. "No," he answered firmly. "Kacey is an old friend of Colt's, and he called for help."

I nodded slowly and glanced back down at the cookie dough. Suddenly, his fingers gripped my chin and turned my face back to his. "Just to clarify before you jump off the conclusion cliff," he said firmly. "You were never a job, and you stopped being a favor the moment we met you. I want to make that clear to you right now."

His face and voice turned deadly serious in seconds, and I felt a shiver run down my spine. There was no doubt that he believed every word he was saying.

"Do you understand what I'm saying?" he asked me as we stood there, locked in a gaze.

"I think so," I whispered, my voice barely audible.

"Forget about Kacey's involvement. If we had been in that park and met you, and we found out you were in danger, we would have still done this, without any calls from Kacey or anyone else. We would have still chosen to protect you. Because it's you," he said, his voice full of conviction.

I frowned at his wording. "What do you mean 'it's me'?"

He smiled softly and released my chin again. "I'm sure you will understand in time."

He nodded to himself and then went back to spooning dough and rolling it into balls and onto the baking sheet, and suddenly it's as though the conversation never even occurred. I just stared at him confused until he picked up one of the sheets and asked me to open the oven for him, jolting me back into focus.

Once we had that batch baking we kept scooping dough onto a second baking tray until all the mixture was gone and we could then swap over trays in the oven. Setting the already cooked batch to cool while we cleaned up the mess we made. The smell of baked cookies had now completely overtaken the kitchen and was making my mouth water and I was so very close to begging Hunt to steal one of the cookies.

Once we had the second batch cooling he picked up one of the already cool cookies and broke it in half, biting into one half while he held out the other half to me. When I went to take it from him with my hand he playfully pulled it away with a grin causing me to roll my eyes at him and hold my mouth open for the cookie, blushing slightly.

Let's face it, the cookies did smell divine and I was probably willing to do a lot more for a taste of one after being surrounded by the smell of them for so long.

He placed the piece of cookie in my mouth, his fingers lingering a few seconds on my lip before he pulled it away and I almost melted at the taste. Of both the cookie and his skin.

I couldn't quite stop the moan that came from me as I savored the cookie and I heard his breath hitch at the sound.

Grinning, I turned and grabbed a cookie myself and broke it in half and offered him one of the halves the same way he did with me. His grin stretched wide as he leaned over and enclosed the cookie in his mouth. Along with the tip of my fingers.

He gave a sharp nip to my fingers before retreating with another grin and I was left there stunned again. And hot. And ever so slightly wet.

Fuck, I definitely lost a competition I didn't even know I was playing at.

He let out a chuckle as he circled around me while I stood there, still as a statue, before he paused at the door to turn and look back at me. His eyes twinkle with amusement as he spoke, "So, what chick flick are you subjecting me to?"

I let out a laugh, but his words jolted me back to reality and I raced after him into the living room. I scoured through the options and settled on the cheesiest chick flick I could find, then stretched out across one of the couches, getting comfortable. Hunt set up the movie, then chose the same couch that I was occupying, lifting my legs and sliding under them before returning them to his lap. I tried to voice a protest, but it was cut off by a soft moan as he massaged my calf muscles with his skilled fingers. He smirked at my reaction but remained focused on the screen in front of us.

Soon, we were both deeply engrossed in the movie, and even though Hunt complained about it being a chick flick, he was more invested in the couple on the screen finding their happily ever after than I was. But then, it wasn't like I hadn't already seen the movie many times before, and it wasn't like I had spent almost the entire length of the movie just watching his reactions to it. Not at all.

Chapter 9

Alexis

After the movie ended, we engaged in casual conversation about our preferences in movies, music, and other miscellaneous topics to get to know each other better. As we sat on the couch, facing each other more directly, the gradually dimming room added a layer of intimacy to the atmosphere. However, feeling the need to delve deeper into more serious topics, I redirected our conversation towards more meaningful subject matter.

"So, I know you told me what your team does in a round-about way, what do you do specifically?" I asked curiously.

"I like firing my gun at people." He playfully waggled his eyebrows at me, causing me to snort with laughter.

I couldn't resist smacking his arm where it rested on the back of the lounge and exclaiming, "I'm serious!"

He responded with a gasp, placing a hand over his chest as though deeply offended that I didn't believe him. "But I am serious," he protested, his grin stretching ear to ear and my laughter intensifying. "Don't I look serious to you?"

I shook my head, still giggling. "No, not even a little bit."

As he waggled his head, chuckling at his own joke, his expression quickly shifted to a more solemn one. "Joking aside," he began in a lower tone, "I am actually the team's gun specialist and sharpshooter."

My jaw dropped in admiration before I burst into another fit of laughter, so uncontrollable that I ended up falling off the couch. It took me a moment to compose myself before I finally managed to blurt out, "You really were being serious!"

He shrugged nonchalantly, his smirk now tinged with seriousness. "Not everyone is as they seem," he said cryptically, and in that moment, the humor that had been present just seconds before vanished.

He seemed to realize his slip of the tongue too late as I said "Yeah, I can definitely attest to that."

I heard him mumble a quick 'Fuck' before he pulled me back onto the couch again.

"Ok, so where was I? Oh yes, Gabe." he said.

As he flashed me another grin, I couldn't help but feel grateful for his ability to deftly steer the conversation away from the previous serious topic. I allowed myself to appreciate his quick and effective redirection.

"Gabe likes blowing shit up," said a voice from behind us.

I looked up at the voice to see the man in question turn on the light before he sauntered into the living room to sit on the couch adjacent to ours.

I gave a half laugh, unsure of whether to take him seriously or not. "Blowing shit up?"

He grinned at me while his brother snickered beside me.

"Gabe is our explosives expert, so yeah, he likes blowing things up." Hunt confirmed.

I turned to Gabe with a wide-eyed expression, and he simply shrugged in response, causing me to tilt my head as I considered the words. After a brief moment of contemplation, I nodded in agreement. "Yeah, I can totally see that," I said.

With a booming laugh, Gabe turned back to Hunt to ask, "So have you told her about Rome and Colt, or were we the first on the list?"

Hunt grinned in response, saying, "Just us so far."

He hummed and shifted to get more comfortable in his seat, lifting his legs up to lie down with his head propped up against the arm. "Rome, how to explain Rome."

Hunt gave a low laugh as he looked back at his brother. "We are only dealing with job descriptions here bro."

I raised my eyebrow at him in question and he just smirked at me.

Gabe nodded in response before he continued. "Rome is essentially a master hacker, capable of accessing and manipulating almost anything on the internet. The term 'hacker' doesn't even begin to do justice to Rome's abilities."

As Gabe stretched his arms over his head, his shirt lifted up slightly to reveal a tantalizing strip of smooth, tattooed skin. My attention was briefly captured by the sight, but fortunately, he wasn't looking at me at the time, so I didn't feel too embarrassed.

Hunt however, reached over and wiped his thumb against the corner of my mouth, his eyes sparked mischievously as he said,. "There was just a little drool there, sweetheart."

I felt my face flush with embarrassment and annoyance as I shoved my hand hard against his chest, sending him falling back against the cushion with laughter. Gabe watched the exchange with a knowing smirk on his face, seemingly amused by the banter between us.

"And Colt?"

Yes, distraction was a great tactic. And denial was my middle name.

"Oooooo, our fearless leader!" Hunt was still laughing at me as he straightened back up.

Gabe hummed, still smirking at us. "So apart from being the drummer that creates the beat we march to, he is an expert in multiple forms of martial arts and hand-to-hand combat," He explained with a hint of admiration in his voice. "He's also the one that pulled our team together."

He didn't elaborate any further but my curiosity didn't want to just leave it like that.

"So, how did you become a team?" I asked.

They glanced at each other briefly, their expressions sobering up very quickly and I almost regretted asking the question based on their looks alone.

Hunt was the one that answered me and the whole atmosphere in the lounge room changed with each word he got out.

"We can't really tell you their stories except to say we all met at one time or another while we served. Both of us were in a bad head space when Colt approached us. He had already left the military at that point. We had enlisted straight out of school and when we both demonstrated a strong affinity in our specialties it came to the attention of some not so nice people who decided to take advantage of our skills for their own purposes. Some of the things we did for them really fucked with our heads."

Hunt's attention drifted downwards as he started fiddling with the stitching on the cushion beneath his fingers, lost in thought.

"Colt had met us in passing just before he finished in the military and being the very perceptive person that he is, he picked up on what was happening. It wasn't long after that when he showed up to get us to join him and Rome."

As Hunt spoke, Gabe shifted his gaze towards us, his eyes betraying a deep sadness that seemed to strike at the very core of my being. Part of me felt an intense curiosity about their past, but the other part of me hesitated, not wanting to pry into painful memories that were clearly still raw for them.

"In all honesty Colt saved our lives the day he came for us. I'm not sure how much longer either of us would have been able to continue in the life we were living. He literally pulled us from the depths of hell."

My heart ached as I watched the emotions play out on their faces. Gabe's sadness had turned into a smile, but it was bittersweet, and Hunt's pain was still evident even as he tried to mask it. I couldn't help but feel a deep desire to comfort him, to take away his pain and make everything better. I wanted to wrap this normally over the top happy man in my arms and tell him that he would never feel that sort of pain again. It had only been four days since I met these men, but already they had become so important to me. I was already so invested in them that I would happily turn the world upside down to never see that sadness in their eyes again.

The anger and hatred that I felt for Dominick is nothing compared to the flash of rage I felt on behalf of Gabe and Hunt.

Without thinking, I found myself on my knees on the couch, my arms wrapped tightly around Hunt. I wanted to tell him that everything would be okay, that he didn't have to feel that pain anymore. As I held him, he slowly responded, his arms wrapping around me as he buried his head in my chest.

Gabe, who had been watching us with a serious expression gave it a minute before he allowed a smile to touch his lips. "You realize he is totally copping a feel of your tits right now right?" he asked, and I could tell he was trying to lighten the mood.

I laughed, grateful for the change in subject. Hunt stayed where he was but held one of his arms out to flip Gabe the bird, but he then sighed and moved back to settle against his corner of the couch again. Humor had returned to his face but I could still see a touch of that sadness lingering in his eyes.

I decided to leave the conversation at that and offer a distraction. "How about we watch another movie and I'll even let you pick this time."

He took the bait and before I knew it we were watching some strange cross between action and comedy featuring The Rock, who Gabe and Hunt argued about being the best of all time. I snickered and made my argument for Jason Statham and watched the good natured banter and argument ensue.

Chapter 10

Alexis

It was midmorning on the fifth day when Hunt dragged me out the back of the house with an arm linked through mine.

I hadn't actually been out there before and I was surprised with how nice it was. I did remember Colt's rule to never be out here without one of them though. The whole area was a canvas of green trees and forest. There was only a small area around the house itself that was clear.

I could hear the trees moving with the wind while the scent of them surrounded us. The feel of the sun directly against my skin felt like magic, like actual fingers of warmth brushing against my skin where it touched.

Hunt dragged me over to where a table was set up at the edge of the house where I could see parts of what I could tell was a gun laid out. Once we were standing behind it, he turned with a serious expression on his face.

"Soooo, Kacey said you know how to shoot, but he didn't really elaborate on if you just know to aim and pull the trigger or if you can actually shoot a target." he said.

I knew there was a question in there somewhere but I couldn't help but tease. "Hunt, are you asking me if I know how to handle a gun?"

He reacted with a slight widening of the eyes to the double entendre before a half-smirk appeared on his face. "Yes, this is me asking if you know how to handle a gun."

I wore a grin on my face as I replied, "I know enough."

"Well, I need to see that you do know. We don't exactly have a gun range here, but I did find a bottle that's over there on that stump. Now, do I need to show you how to assemble and take apart this pretty little gun here or can you muddle through on your own?" He was still smirking at me and his voice was challenging.

I was totally there for a good challenge.

I let out a laugh in response and flicked my hand at him in a motion to move away from the weapon. He eagerly complied, practically skipping a few steps back and then turned to make exaggerated hand gestures, as if he were a presenter on a game show.

I had a quick look at the pieces of the weapon on the table and took a moment to breathe and center myself. Then I got started... Well, when I say started, it didn't really take all that long. I didn't really time myself, and I wasn't sure if Hunt did, but I knew my average was about twenty-two seconds from start to shoot... not including disassembling the gun again, and I obviously was working with an unfamiliar gun so who could blame me if I slipped a little. My fair guess was still around the half a minute mark before I heard the bottle shattering as my bullet hit it.

I quickly disassembled the gun again and returned the parts to their starting places before I turned to look at Hunt.

He stared at me and the gun, alternating his gaze between the two, his eyes wide and his mouth slightly open. After a few moments of this, he blinked and snapped his mouth shut, coughing slightly to clear his throat. "Fuck, that was hot," he said, his eyes still fixed on me.

I gave a startled laugh and raised my eyebrows at his declaration, to which he simply shrugged in response.

"What? I say it like I see it, and that, sweetheart, just made my cock hard." he declared.

His words drew my attention downward where I could clearly see he was telling the truth. I felt a slight flush creep onto my cheeks, so I looked away again back towards the tree line. I felt him move into my space and he briefly touched my chin to return my gaze to him.

He was a lot closer now and his eyes and hair gleamed in the sun. "In all seriousness though, you know we like you right?"

I blinked at him in surprise. "We? As in you and–?"

He gave me a soft smile. "We, as in all of us. All four of us are very much attracted to you."

I furrowed my brows and tilted my head, unsure of what to say. "But I could never choose between you. I would never want to come between your team."

Hunt shook his head, a small smile on his lips. "You wouldn't be," he said.

"What do you mean?" I asked with a frown.

"I mean we would never make you choose. You could be with all of us, together," he responded, continuing to look at me with a soft smile.

My breathing stopped for a moment. "Umm, what?"

He chuckled and stepped closer. His finger traced down my throat and collarbone, causing a jolt of electricity to shoot through me. I never knew such a simple touch could have that sort of effect on a woman's body, but I could feel his gentle brush of fingers everywhere.

"We're a team, sweetheart. We've been together for a long time and spend a lot of time in close quarters. We're not like normal brothers who can't share, we like to share. A lot," he whispers.

I felt like air was a luxury I couldn't afford right at that point as Hunt's hand played with the loose strand of hair at the nape of my neck that had fallen from my hair tie. I felt a rush of heat spread through my body and I panted softly, the thought of being shared truly by them entered my mind for the first time and ignited a fire deep inside me.

"I've seen how you look at us, Lexi, I know you feel this connection between us too." He continued as though I was not internally losing my mind.

"I..." My mind went blank as Hunt's lips softly touched mine, erasing whatever words I had on the tip of my tongue. I could feel his eyes on me as he repeated the action, brushing his lips against mine with delicate touches. It was a gentle, almost fleeting kiss that sent shivers down my spine. I couldn't help but close my eyes and part my lips, returning the affection with a growing hunger.

He took advantage of the green light and intensified the kiss from a mere two to an explosive twenty-two. He clasped the nape of my neck, pressing his lips onto mine with a possessive and devastating hold. His tongue entwined with mine, while his other hand clutched my hip firmly. I couldn't help but moan into his mouth, gripping his shirt with both hands. I barely held back from attacking him like a wild animal. Suddenly, he eased the kiss down to a soft caress, pulling away from me slowly. His hot breath fanned over my lips, leaving them pulsing and tingling.

He flashed a mischievous grin and released me, taking a few steps back around the side of the table. As though space could quell the intense inferno he ignited.

"Sooooo, where did you learn to shoot?" he asked nonchalantly, as though he hadn't just rocked my proverbial world.

I felt like I was getting whiplash but I did appreciate the change in topic to calm my raging hormones and allow myself time to process what the fuck just happened.

"When I was still recovering from what happened I couldn't do much in the way of physical exercise, but I could learn how to shoot a gun and everything that came with it. One of the ladies at my therapy group was ex-military. After she heard my story she started taking me to a range almost every day until she was happy with my very thorough knowledge and use." I shrugged, trying to pass it off as though it was no big deal, when in reality it meant so much to me.

Something must have shown on my face because in the next moment he smiled at me softly and asked, "I gather from this look on your face that she is a good friend now?"

"My best friend." I said with a laugh.

"And you're sure the leak didn't come from her?"

A wave of anger washed over me before I pushed it away. I knew it was a logical question and I can't fault him for asking. I understood the need to question everything.

"No, there isn't a chance. Besides the part where she never actually knew my real name because I was never allowed to tell her, she was the kind of friend who would kill for me rather than sell me out."

Hunt chuckled, "Those types of friends are the best to have, aren't they?"

As I think about my friend, my smile widened, and I expressed, "If either of us were into girls, I would have definitely wifed her ass months ago and not be in the situation I find myself in now." Laughing, I glanced down at the gun pieces on the table.

Suddenly, his hands pulled me back around to face him, and I realized that he had moved closer while I wasn't paying attention, yet he still maintained a safe distance.

"The situation? You mean the situation where you have four men who are interested in getting to know you? The real you and not just the persona created by the US Marshal Service?"

His face appeared genuine and it made my heart skip a beat. Suddenly, he changed his tone and said, "Or maybe you just mean the situation where all four of those guys want to fuck you."

I was caught off guard and laughed, and he grinned before letting me go to pick up the gun pieces and reassemble them. After handing it to me with the safety on and a box of ammunition, he became serious.

"Carry it with you at all times. Hopefully you won't need to use it, but it's essential to have it in case of an emergency," he instructed.

It was an unexpected end to our conversation.

But it was probably for the best. Ignoring that my body felt like a slow burning fire had been lit from within, my thoughts were a chaotic mess, swirling with everything that had transpired since we left the house. I had been yearning for the validation that the attraction was mutual, and now that Hunt had confirmed it, along with the fact that I don't have to make a choice between the four men, my mind was in overdrive trying to process the new information.

Chapter 11

Gabe

There was just something about her.

In a word she was amazing. She was truly remarkable and I couldn't fathom why anyone would want to harm her. However, we were determined to prevent that from happening again.

She had established a daily routine for herself. Right now we knew she was going to be in the gym for a couple of hours doing her regular run or working out on the weights or machines. Once she finished with that we knew she would help whoever had dinner duty, and then after dinner she would curl up on the lounge near us watching a movie or playing one of the games with us.

We picked up on her aversion to darkness straight away so one of us would always make sure to turn on the lights for her at the first sign of her anxiety creeping in along with the night. She had slotted into our routines like she had always been a part of us.

Which is why we took the opportunity to meet in the office while she was busy in the gym to discuss any relevant progress or updates. Like we did every couple of days. We were thankful that this office was large and we weren't cramped. But despite the comfort of the chairs, I chose to lean against the wall.

Probably my anxiety and frustration bleeding through my calm.

We couldn't just ignore the outside world as much as I would have liked to. So, therefore, we did need to keep on top of anything of importance. Like the hunt for the asshole Dominick.

Or the voicemail that Rome had retrieved from her messagebank earlier that day that was now playing for us to hear.

"I need to know if you're okay hun. Your major marshal asswipe isn't telling me shit and I'm really worried. Call me back so I know you're alive before I start hunting your cute ass down."

The voice was feminine and you could hear the frustration and worry in it. I could see Colt frowning as the recording came to an end, his attention distracted.

"What's the matter?" I inquired, my eyes narrowed as I tried to assess the situation.

Colt started to respond, but then shook his head, dismissing whatever seemed to trouble him about the voicemail. I'm certain that if it were relevant or important, he would assess it again later.

"That must be her best friend," Hunt chimed in, also frowning in the direction of the computer. "She mentioned her to me when we spoke earlier today, but I didn't realize she knew Kacey."

Colt looked at him curiously. "What did she say about her?"

"She said they're best friends," Hunt answered. "That she had a military background. They met while Lexi was going through therapy because of what Dominick did to her. Because of that, she took Lexi under her wing and taught her how to shoot." He shrugged, but I could tell from the gleam in his eye that there was more to this information, or perhaps to the conversation he had with Lexi in general.

I exchanged glances with Colt and Rome. We all knew Hunt enough to recognise that gleam, it was just a matter of who asked the questions.

I sighed and took the bait.

"So? How did your lesson go? Did you get to, what was it you said, 'wrap your arms around her rocking body to show her the correct technique'?" I drawled at him, already knowing I'm just encouraging him, and when I saw his grin turn almost manic I knew I was right.

"Brother, you should have seen it, it was a thing of beauty." He snickered almost to himself.

Colt rolled his eyes at my brother's antics. "Yes, we already know she is a thing of beauty, now get to the point." I could see Colt losing his patience and I forced myself not to laugh at his expense. He should have known better when dealing with Hunt.

"I don't mean Lexi herself, though yes she is a thing of beauty and her mouth is pure sin," he held up a hand as on cue we all opened our mouths to say something about that particular tidbit. "I'll come back to that. But what I'm talking about is the fact that I watched her assemble, shoot a bottle dead center at fifty yards, and then disassemble the gun with no guidance or instructions."

I was impressed, and I could see that the others were too. It meant she had at least a decent knowledge of guns and may be able to partially hold her own if need be.

"In under a minute…"

My eyes widened as one of the others mumbles 'Fuck'. Yeah I could see the reason behind the manic grin now. If there was anything that Hunt was truly passionate about, it was his guns. They allowed him to escape his own thoughts the same way working on explosives did to me.

Rome smirked at me. "She's faster than you."

I flipped him the bird by way of a scratch to my eyebrow and he just laughed.

I'm still distracted though because Hunt was an asshole sometimes and liked to drag out torture. "Can we backtrack a little bit now. Umm, 'her mouth is pure sin'? You can't not explain that one."

He cackled, because he knew it would torture me, he slipped that in on purpose.

Once he had settled down again at Colt's glare he held his hands up in surrender. "Ok, fine. You guys always ruin my fun. Anyway, I may have had a conversation with her about how we all may be feeling a certain way towards her."

Rome narrowed his eyes and looked at me. "Do you mind if I kill him? I could source some really good poison and make it painless. You won't miss him that much right?"

Hunt gave an exaggerated gasp and clutched at his chest dramatically. "You wound me. And here I thought we were brothers."

Rome scoffed and pointed at me with a straight face as I rubbed a hand across my mouth in an effort to try to hide a grin at their banter. "No, he's your brother, I just tolerate you." He then smirks, letting Hunt know that he isn't serious.

Colt had his head rested in his hands in an effort to ignore us. "I swear I'm surrounded by children."

I raised my eyebrow at Hunt, still not allowing myself to get distracted. "And? I hope you didn't fuck it up for us."

Hunt sobered up and bit into his lip, and I was instantly filled with dread. If he fucked it up I'd be absolutely supporting Rome's plan to kill him. I opened my mouth to say just that but he shushed me with a waved hand. He looked truly offended as only a brother could.

"Do you really think I'd do anything to mess it up for us? We all have a connection to her, not just you, not just me. I approached the conversation carefully, considering all of us," he said.

I opened my mouth only to be shushed again by Colt much to my annoyance. "And? What was her reaction?"

"Her first concern was that she didn't want to choose between us or come between us, metaphorically speaking," he replied, smirking. "But when she thought about coming between us in a more physical sense and being shared by us, I thought she was going to spontaneously combust."

The teasing bastard.

Colt gave him an annoyed look. "So that's when you decided you could have a taste?"

He chuckled. "Maybe. Like I said, pure fucking sin." He groaned and closed his eyes, obviously reliving the moment in his mind.

Colt rolled his eyes again, but I could see the desire in his gaze for the beautiful brunette in the other room.

A glint came to Hunt's eyes again, his smile stretched further. "I can't wait to cuddle up to her again tonight after what we did earlier."

Colt's lips twitched. "Looks like you'll have to wait a little longer. You'll be sleeping in your own bed tonight. You've already had four nights to cuddle up to her, so I'm sure you can handle a night alone."

I almost burst out laughing at Colt's ultimate revenge and the puppy-dog look on Hunt's face.

The humor quickly faded from Hunt's face as he frowned back at Colt. "But what about her nightmares?"

Colt threw a grin my way, and I knew he was about to stir shit up. "I'm sure your brother is just as capable of offering comfort as you are."

I couldn't help but laugh as Hunt got up and stomped out of the office, grumbling about betrayal and being personally attacked.

Colt gave into the humor he was trying to disguise so as not to encourage Hunt, laughing as he said, "Well, I guess that means the meeting is over."

A grin stretched across my face. Yeah I guess it was too.

Chapter 12

Alexis

When I woke up this time it's thankfully only with a whimper instead of a full scream. There was a hand rubbing along my arm while the person it belonged to made soft sounds of comfort. At first I thought that it was Hunt in my bed again as he had been since the first night, but when I looked over I could see straight away from the light shining from the closet that there was ink stretching across most of his skin. And the scent of something spicy reached me that I associated with Gabe.

Great, they seemed to be taking turns to have their sleep constantly interrupted to try to help me with my nightmares.

I shook away my depressive thoughts as Gabe watched me from where he was lying on his side facing me, still resting a hand on my upper arm in comfort. I rolled towards him to lie on my side facing him in turn, grabbing his hand with one of my own as he went to take it back at my movement. He squeezed my fingers in response but let me clutch at it.

"Hi, I'm sorry if I woke you." My voice was soft in the stillness of the night.

He responded by gently shaking his head and said, "Don't apologize for having nightmares. We have all been there at some time or another. We all know what it's like."

I raised my eyebrow at him and he just shook his head again in response to my silent question, letting me know it's not for discussion at that moment.

"Besides, I would never complain about sharing a bed with you," his whispered confession brought a blush to my cheeks.

I admitted, "When I woke up, I thought it was Hunt in the bed. He had been sleeping here for the past few nights, but I suppose he needs some undisturbed rest tonight."

Feeling slightly bashful, I lowered my head and focused my attention on our clasped hands resting between us.

Gabe let out a soft scoff in response, "Don't worry about Hunt. He wanted to be here, and if you even hint that you want him back, he'll come running. But for tonight, he's been sent to his own bed."

His statement caused me to furrow my brows in confusion. "You sent your own brother away?"

Gabe grinned widely and shook his head, glancing away from me towards a slouched figure in the armchair. I followed his gaze and saw Colt, slouched in the chair with his elbow resting on the arm and his head propped up by his hand, fast asleep.

Gabe looked back at me with a glint in his eyes and said, "Did you really think he wouldn't keep watch over you?"

I hummed in acknowledgement, a small smile forming on my lips as I lowered my head again.

We lapsed into a comfortable silence, lost in our own contemplations. After a while, Gabe broke the quiet. "I know

Hunt spoke to you about this connection we feel," he said, his voice low and steady. I was taken aback by his sudden confession and glanced up at him with wide eyes, but his expression was open and non-judgmental.

Gabe's lips curved into a gentle smile. "There is nothing that happens individually that we don't all know about eventually," he continued, "communication and honesty are extremely important to make a team like ours work, both professionally and personally." I nodded my head in agreement, understanding the significance of trust and transparency in a close-knit team like theirs.

He looked at me expectantly. "Are you okay with what Hunt discussed with you?" Gabe asked, giving me a chance to voice my thoughts.

I considered his words for a moment, letting them sink in. Taking into account his emphasis on communication and honesty, I decided to speak my mind.

I let out a small sigh before speaking, my voice barely above a whisper. Gabe's attention was on me, his eyes softened with concern. "I'm a little scared," I confessed, my words barely audible in the quiet room.

He tilted his head slightly, his expression growing more serious. "About what?" he asked gently, his hand still resting comfortingly in mine.

I took a deep breath, steeling myself to voice my fears. "I'm scared that this connection we have is just because of the intense situation we're in. That once everything is over, you won't want me like that anymore."

Gabe's frown deepened as he considered my words. "You need to understand," he began, his voice low and serious.

"Although we've been with other women and have shared other women, we've never felt this instant connection before. None of us have. This feeling we all have with you has never happened to us before, and that's not just because of the situation we're in. We're experienced enough to know that the feeling won't go away when the situation does."

He watched me closely as I absorbed his words, giving me space to think about what he'd said. "Do you understand? Are you okay with that?" he whispered, his tone gentle and tentative.

I nodded slowly, a weight lifting from my chest as I realized that they feel the same way I do. It was a relief to know that my feelings were reciprocated, and the small smile that tugged at my lips was genuine.

"Does that mean I can kiss you now?" he asked softly and I released a quiet giggle. "I've wanted to kiss you for days and my asshole brother got there first."

His question lingered in the air, heavy with desire. I could feel his warm breath ghosting over my lips as he waited for my answer. I couldn't help the soft giggle that escaped my lips at his confession. I nodded. Without another word, he leaned in, and I could feel the softness of his lips against mine. I breathed in sharply at the contact and I felt his own lips stretch in a small smile as he continued to brush them against mine. It was gentle and tentative at first, as if he was testing the waters, and I found myself wanting more. As our lips moved together, I felt a jolt of electricity shoot through me, and my heart began to race. The touch of cool metal against my lip from his lip piercing created a different sensation before he flicked the tip of his tongue against my lips, encouraging me to open for him. I gave in instantly and his tongue swept in to tangle with mine. The cold hardness of a tongue piercing surprised me and I gasped into the kiss. As our kiss deepened, his hand released mine, and I felt his fingers grip my hip, pulling me closer to him.

He had his tongue fucking pierced. The sensation sent shivers down my spine. My thoughts then moved to where else he might have pierced and I couldn't control the soft moan that left me at those thoughts.

He chuckled huskily into the kiss as he slowed it back down and brought it to a stop, moving away from me again. The smile he gave me was all sex. "To be continued when you don't need more sleep and we aren't risking waking the boss man."

My eyes darted quickly to the armchair with Colt in it, he hadn't moved, still sleeping deeply from the look of it.

Gabe rolled onto his back and he drew me to tuck into his side, the same way his brother does, as he whispered for me to go to sleep. Both of us shut our eyes and snuggled into more comfortable positions, my head tucked onto his chest and my hand holding his once again in comfort.

I briefly blinked my eyes open again and caught the gleam of the light reflected in Colt's eyes. He hadn't moved at all, not even a twitch, but his eyes were open and watching us. Our eyes connected and a slow smile crossed his lips, telling me silently that he had been awake the whole time.

Chapter 13

Alexis

"So I said to him, 'Nathan, if you hurt that other boy then you should know you're going to get into trouble. Even if he did take your toy you cannot just bite him to get it back.'"

Sam had returned with her pine scent trailing behind her. She had come in just after breakfast with a coffee cake and a pat to my cheek.

And she brought fresh clothes. She was officially my domestic goddess.

After she did her routine of tidying and clothes collections she pulled me into the dining area for a coffee and a slice of cake just like her last visit.

I giggled at her story about her son that she was retelling using wild hand gestures. So much that she almost knocked over her coffee cup at least three times.

"How did he respond?" I gasped out.

"He stood there with his hands on his little hips and his little feet apart and he goes, 'but mummy you bite Daddy sometimes when he takes things from you.'" The artificial frown on her face disappeared into laughter. "I mean, what can I say to something like that! I told him to go sit in his room and think about what he did wrong, and after he stomped away and slammed his door as best as his little arms could do, I then laughed and laughed until I almost peed myself!"

We started giggling uncontrollably once more.

"It sounds like there is far too much fun going on over here." Hands landed on my shoulders startling me and I jolted in my seat in surprise.

I hadn't been paying attention and glancing up at the face leaning over my shoulder, I was able to see that it was Hunt that had snuck up on us. I honestly shouldn't have been surprised as I knew he took great pleasure in sneaking up on people.

He grinned and pressed a small kiss to my temple before he grabbed my fork and stole a chunk of my coffee cake.

"Hey!" I smacked his hand and stole my fork back from him as he laughed. "You wouldn't like it if I retaliated like Nathan did to the little boy who stole his toy."

I think about what I said for only a moment. On second thought, maybe he would.

He looked at Sam with a raised eyebrow and she made a dramatic imitation of chomping her teeth in his direction. He looked back at me with a raised eyebrow and a sly grin, telling me my thoughts were spot on.

Heat crept up my neck that I hoped went unnoticed by both of them.

He chuckled as he started wandering towards the kitchen. "Would either of you beautiful ladies like a refill?"

Sam giggled again but pushed herself up and out of her chair. "As lovely as that sounds, I need to go pick up my naughty boy and take him home."

Hunt nodded and smiled in response before continuing on into the kitchen.

The moment he was past the doorway Sam rounded on me with round eyes and a grin before whispering rapidly. "Umm, hello? You seem to have neglected to tell me something."

I laughed and ducked my head. There was no way that I was talking about any of the complicated situations I found myself in, no matter how much I enjoyed her company.

She nodded to herself as though it's a foregone conclusion and said, "Okay, next time I'm here you have to tell me all about what is going on between you and that beautiful happy man-meat in there."

Oh, if only she knew. But nope, she never will.

I waved her off and she left just as quietly as she appeared. I turned to find Hunt leaning casually against the kitchen doorway watching me with a smile stretched across his face and a glint of mischief in his eye.

Admittedly, there wasn't anything new about that, it was a look I was becoming familiar with, but now I wondered what thoughts were behind that look. And would I be allowed to kiss that smile on his face?

My indecision must have shown as he crooked a finger at me, saying, "Come over here sweetheart."

I grinned and ambled over to where he was standing and he cupped my face with both hands, he leant down and brushed his lips softly against mine.

It was gentle and made me hum in happiness at him. He didn't push for more and just wrapped his arms around me in a solid hug. It settled something inside me. Just being wrapped in his arms gave me comfort. But it was only brief and before I knew it he was then stepping back and brushing a hand against my cheek.

"I'm sorry I wasn't there when you woke up during the night." he said, and I could see that it had clearly been troubling him a little.

I chuckled as I remembered. "I heard you were sent to your room like a naughty boy," I responded.

He grinned at me, losing the momentary somber look. "If only," he scoffed before softening again. "I heard Gabe was there for you, though."

I felt the blush spread across my cheeks as I dipped my head and gave him a slight nod. "Yeah."

He tilted my chin back up. "Don't be embarrassed, I'm glad he was there for you, sweetheart. I hope he made you feel better."

I smiled at the memory. "He did."

Hunt nodded in response, accepting my answer. "Good," he said with a hint of amusement. "I can let him keep living his best life then."

I couldn't help but chuckle at his playful remark.

He brushed his lips against mine again. Deepening the kiss briefly he slid his tongue in to tangle with mine for a moment before he retreated again and stepped back. "Are you heading for your workout?"

I laughed, "Am I that predictable?"

He simply grinned in return before turning me around and nudged me in the direction of the gym.

Then he smacked my ass.

I gasped as my hand went to my now hot asscheek and I looked back at him over my shoulder. The look on his face was playful and all I could do was shake my head at him in amusement and continue towards the gym and my regularly scheduled workout.

Spending the next few hours working out helped settle me and clear my mind again. After finishing my workout, I made my way through the dining space towards the kitchen. As I passed by the dining table, my eyes fell upon Rome's computer, left unattended with its screen displaying a flurry of activity. Curiosity got the better of me, I took a quick peek at the different windows and tabs that seemed to be working away on something, all without the presence of their owner.

I continued to make my way towards the kitchen for a glass of water and as I entered the kitchen I found Rome already in there filling up a glass for himself from the chilled filter tap while he looked out the window into the trees, the sun shining off the different browns in his hair.

"How was your workout?" he inquired without turning to face me.

I'm baffled as to how he knew I was there, given that he hadn't moved from his spot by the window. And how did he know I had just finished exercising? It seems that I've become predictable, and perhaps it's time for me to alter my routine.

Finally, he glanced my way as he placed the brimming glass on the counter. I noticed his eyes darting down my body, scanning my workout attire.

I came to a stop behind him near the other side of the kitchen, waiting for my turn to get some water. "It was good."

He turned towards me fully and leaned back against the counter, crossing his arms across his chest, and looked to be deep in thought about something. "I know you have kissed the twins, and I know they have both explained to you how we work."

Well, okay then, let's just dive right in shall we.

His tone was very serious and his eyes were assessing, taking in every expression and movement of my body. I'd never been so acutely conscious of each tiny interaction as I was with him. Rome possessed an uncanny ability to shift from laughter to a serious, intense demeanor in the span of a single breath, and it was as if being in his presence was akin to taking a ride on a roller coaster.

But then I did always love riding roller coasters.

He continued, "I want you to really think about this before you just throw yourself headfirst into a relationship with us. We aren't all sunshine and rainbows. We all have our own demons and they generally come out to play in the bedroom in various ways."

I could feel a smile playing on my lips as I arched an eyebrow at him. "Do you really believe that would scare me off? I think you have me confused with someone else. You should know by now that I'm not a delicate flower. I can handle whatever you throw my way."

Leaving the glass of water he just poured on the counter behind him, he strode towards me, his presence like a looming dark cloud. Despite my determination not to back down, I found myself taking a step back as he approached, until my back hit the kitchen cabinets behind me. The cold wood made me flinch, and his hands reached out to rest against my hips. It was the first time he had touched me, and although his grip was firm, there was a surprising gentleness to his touch. His subtle scent washed over me, faintly reminiscent of chocolate, and my mouth watered in response.

As his thumbs traced gentle circles on my hip bones, he hummed in a low, seductive tone. His voice sent shivers down my spine, as if he was caressing my bare skin with a feather-light touch.

"Are you absolutely certain you want to play with me, Lexi? I'm not like the others. My tastes are... different," he murmured, his voice soft and husky, and it moved through me as though he was sliding a finger along my bare skin.

It took a moment for me to process his words, but when I did, I felt a spark of excitement ignite within me.

So, this was really about him. Well, I was definitely intrigued now.

"Oh, I'm *very* sure." Well, after what he said I wasn't actually completely sure, but I refused to back down now, dammit. And how bad could it possibly be?

His hands slid ever so slowly up my sides, his thumbs offering feather light touches to my ribs, and then the undersides of my breasts, taking a path up their sides instead of over my too tight nipples that were now aching for his attention.

He suddenly used a slight pressure to ever so slowly raise my arms above my head. His hands softly continued their path upward until they were braced against my wrists.

"Such soft, pretty little wrists. They would look so much prettier tied to my headboard." The rasp of his voice sent a shiver down my spine as he slid his face along the side of mine before he nuzzled into the soft flesh of my neck.

Well, fuck.

His tongue flicked out against the sensitive skin just below my ear, making me moan. He slowly feathered kisses and he nibbled at the skin of my jawline.

He continued to offer soft brushes of his lips, never truly making direct contact with where I was panting and desperate for his mouth.

He hovered over me, his mouth only an inch from mine. His tongue finally flicked out to tease against my quivering bottom lip.

"So, you want to be my good girl?"

I whimpered.

I honest to god whimpered for him.

My brain was mush.

A loud beep emanated from his computer in the dining area, prompting a hum from him. His face was so close to mine that I could feel the subtle vibration. He then moved his hands down my arms in a slow, deliberate motion until they were cradling the sides of my face. With a gentle brush of his lips against the corner of my mouth, he whispered, "To be continued."

And then he was disappearing back out to his computer as though he hadn't just left me a panting, shaky, horny mess against the oh so clean kitchen cabinets.

I tried to get my breathing under control again as I stumbled forward towards the glass of water Rome left on the counter, drinking it all as I tried to calm myself down. His scent was still invading my head.

After a moment to compose myself I breezed back out of the kitchen and headed towards the stairs for a shower. A cold one now obviously.

He glanced up at me as I walked past, and I'm sure he saw the slight tremble still affecting me as he offered me a wink.

Despite my efforts to compose myself, my voice still came out slightly breathy as I confessed, "I drank your water, you'll have to get yourself a new one."

He responded with a grin and remarked, "It was meant for you anyway."

Well, okay then.

Chapter 14

Alexis

I must have fallen asleep again while we watched a movie. This time I stirred awake to find myself being lifted up and carried towards my bed. As my eyes fluttered open and then closed again, I caught a brief glimpse of Gabe's colorful tattoos.

His strong arms enveloped me, tightening around my body as he mumbled sweetly, "Hey, beautiful."

I could tell he was being exceedingly careful not to jostle me, with one arm tucked beneath my knees and the other wrapped securely around my back, holding me close to his chest.

I let out a contented hum and snuggled even closer into Gabe's warm embrace as he continued to carry me. Suddenly, I heard the sound of my bedroom door opening and then closing behind us, signaling that we were not alone. Gabe came to a stop, and I heard the rustling of my bedding as he slowly lowered me down onto the bed. The soft sheets glided against my skin as gentle hands began to shift my body into a more comfortable position. I blinked my eyes open again and

I was met with the sight of Hunt before me, the closet light glinting in his hair. "Come over here, sweetheart," he coaxed, drawing me closer to him.

I rolled onto my side and shuffled towards him, expecting for him to roll to his back and drag me in like he normally does but he stayed facing towards me. Moments later the blankets behind me shifted and I tilted back to see Gabe slide in on my other side.

I couldn't hide the humor or the smile that crept onto my face as he curled around my back with an arm flung over my waist. I looked towards the armchair but I already knew it was empty.

Gabe snickered at my look and commented, "We're unsupervised for once. He had a call planned, so he will be in the office for a while."

I expressed a slight frown and asked, "Is everything alright?"

In reply, he nodded and said, "I'm sure he will let you know if anything of importance comes up."

Hunt used his fingers on my jaw to pull my attention back to him. "But while the cat's away and all that..." he waggled his eyebrows at me causing me to chuckle and bite down on my bottom lip.

His expression shifted slightly as his eyes flicked down to where my lip is still caught between my teeth. With his thumb still resting against my jaw, he gently pulled my lip out of my mouth, sliding his thumb along the soft flesh before sliding his hand to the back of my head and drawing my lips to his.

It was a soft kiss at first, like it usually was with Hunt, a gentle brush of his lips against mine. My hand gripped at his side, clutching and pulling in an attempt to draw him even closer to me.

I suddenly felt Gabe's warm lips against the curve of my neck and the unexpected sensation made me gasp, and I'm overwhelmed by the feeling of both of them kissing me at the same time. Hunt took full advantage of my parted lips, deepening our kiss and swallowing the moan that escaped me.

His tongue slid against mine, tangling with it before re-treating and then coming back for more. Gabe's lips were slowly trailing open mouthed kisses up my neck and then to the sensitive flesh at my ear, his tongue darted out to tease at my ear lobe just as his hand slid up from my waist to palm at my breast through the shirt I had on. The gentle squeeze of his hand made me gasp into Hunt's kiss.

I had heard of the term twin sandwich before–I mean who hadn't?--but to actually find myself in the center of one... Wow. If this was what I could expect moving forward being 'shared' between them, sign me the fuck up right now.

Hunt's hand disappeared from my neck but then it trailed softly over my hip and down to the back of my thigh, gripping it and lifting it to wrap around his hip, his own knee pushed between my legs. I could feel his hard length against me.

Gabe's hand that was palming my breast moved up to-wards my jaw. His fingers gripped my face firmly, but not painfully, redirecting my attention to him. He hungrily claimed my lips, replacing the taste of Hunt with himself. I released my grip on Hunt, reaching behind me to tangle my fingers in Gabe's hair, eliciting a shiver from him. He moaned into our kiss, his grip on my jaw intensifying to a point that bordered on pain, but was still enjoyable. I could feel his own hard cock pressing against my ass as he rocked into me.

Kissing them both so close together made their differences even stronger. Gabe's lips consumed me with a fierce intensity, his tongue twirled with mine while the cool metal of his piercings contrasted with the warmth of his mouth.

Hunt shuffled down the bed until his face was level with my chest. He closed his mouth around one hard nipple through my shirt, his teeth pulled at it and made me arch my back, pushing my chest harder into his face as I moaned loudly into Gabe's kiss.

I felt Hunt's fingers tease at the bare skin between my shirt and pants, silently asking me for permission to go further. I used my other hand to move his hand upwards under my shirt until our combined hands dragged it up enough it had to stop for where his mouth was still on my nipple. He released my nipple long enough to shove the shirt the rest of the way up my chest before his mouth moved instantly back, sucking my nipple into his mouth and swirling his tongue around it. His hand surrounded my other breast and squeezed firmly.

Gabe's hand released my jaw and he slid it firmly down my side before coming to a stop at the waistband of my pants, his fingers trailing along it. I reached down and pushed his hand into my pants, and seconds later Gabe's fingers slid through my wetness and brushed over my clit.

Fuck. My pussy was aching for them, pulsing with need. They had taken only moments to stoke the flames of my desire into a raging fire.

We both moaned and my head fell to the mattress as I panted harshly, Gabe's mouth going back to my neck to kiss and nip at the skin there. He rubbed harder against my clit before moving down and using my own wetness to thrust two fingers deep inside me.

I cried out at the feeling of fullness. It had been a long time since I'd had any sexual contact to even this degree. And fuck, it felt so good.

My hips rocked onto his fingers, moving with the slow thrust of them.

Gabe's thumb found my clit again while his fingers continued to move in and out of me. I could feel my climax building rapidly and my pussy started clenching around his fingers. He lifted his head, his eyes watching my face and taking in every twitch, pant, and moan.

"That's it, beautiful, ride my fingers," he murmured as he watched me.

Hunt bit down on the nipple in his mouth and it sent me flying over the edge. Gabe's other hand slid over my mouth before the first cry left it. My pussy pulsed around his fingers and pleasure flooded me like a tidal wave.

Giving one last lick to my nipple Hunt trailed his mouth all the way back up my chest and neck and after moving his brother's hand his mouth devoured mine again.

Releasing my mouth he looked at me with hungry eyes. "Fuck, sweetheart, you are stunning when you cum," he murmured, his voice filled with desire. "I want you so badly right now." A hand trailed up the side of my leg sending a shiver through me.

The sudden sound of someone clearing their throat startled us all, and we all turned towards the door in a flurry of movement. Apparently, we were so caught up in our activities that we hadn't even heard the door open or seen the change in light from the hall. Colt was standing there, his arms crossed over his chest and one eyebrow arched.

"I think it's best if Lexi gets some sleep," he said, his tone amused. "Just like you guys were planning to do an hour ago."

Hunt let out an irritated groan. "Fucking cockblocker."

I chuckled and playfully pushed Hunt back onto the bed with my hand. I quickly adjusted my shirt to cover my chest, noticing the flicker of desire in Colt's eyes as they trail over my skin before I got my shirt straightened.

"Can I trust you all to behave or do I need to send you both to your own beds and take your place?"

My body flushed with heat at his words. Imagining Colt where Hunt and Gabe had been just moments before sent a surge of arousal through me.

Gabe laughed, the movement vibrating through my body, before he nodded to Colt. "We can behave."

He responded with a hum and made his way over to the armchair, which appeared to have become his usual spot for sleeping. "If you don't behave, I'll have to kick you out," he warns with a playful tone.

I propped myself up on my hands to get a better look at him as he settled in. "How was your phone call?" I asked curiously.

He glanced at me with an unusual expression. "It was alright, princess. Let's talk about it tomorrow." He appeared exhausted, and that's why I didn't push it any further and simply nodded in agreement. I fell back onto the bed, but I didn't miss the look of gratitude on his face.

"Get some sleep, princess. You will need it tomorrow."

I started to lift my head again to question him but Gabe chuckled and physically rolled me towards Hunt again before curling around my back, his hand wrapped around my waist to pull me back into him. Hunt ended up rolling onto his stomach with his arms under the pillow and my leg still tangled in his. My hand slid under the pillow to twine with his and he smiled softly without opening his eyes again, my other hand did the same with Gabe's on my waist.

"Sweet dreams, princess," was whispered in a gentle tone, and though I heard it, I was already drifting back to sleep.

That night was the first night I didn't wake from a nightmare since arriving there.

Chapter 15

Alexis

The following morning, I woke up from a restful sleep and realized that Gabe and Hunt had already left. I noticed that the sheets were still warm, indicating that they had left not long before I woke up. Their absence may have been what woke me from my sleep.

Or perhaps it was the sensation of being watched by Colt, who sat in the armchair, elbows on his knees and hands clasped together.

I sat up in bed, resting against the headboard. "Were you watching me sleep?" I asked, my voice was still groggy from sleep.

He shrugged, a small smile played at the corners of his lips. "Maybe."

I let out a soft chuckle, but I knew something was up, he was never normally still there when I woke up. "Is something wrong?"

His forehead creased with a frown for a moment before he looked down at his clasped hands. "There still hasn't been any progress on finding Dominick. It's almost like he vanished into thin air or even left the country. But we know he wouldn't have left." He gives me a meaningful look.

I gave a hum in agreement. "No, he wouldn't have left while I'm still breathing."

Colt tilted his head to the side, studying me. "You seem surprisingly calm about that."

I made a dismissive sound, but then took a moment to think about how to say what I was about to say. "Did you know I died once? Dominick had literally killed me before," I started, my voice steady and not betraying the turmoil I was feeling. "While I was on the emergency room table my heart completely stopped. One of the many times he stabbed me, he punctured my lung and it filled up with blood. I almost choked to death on my own blood but then my heart couldn't deal with the stress and I flatlined for five and a half minutes."

He remained utterly silent while I dredged up the memories of what that man had done to me.

"For a long time, the doctors were unsure if I would fully recover. They even spoke about potential brain damage due to lack of oxygen. I had to attend a lot of physical and mental therapy in an attempt to move past what happened. And at the same time I was also all alone being hidden in a completely strange city with a whole new identity to remember, because I could no longer live the life I had been living. Hell, my parents still think I died that day."

He watched me with a sad expression, but didn't interrupt as I spoke at my own pace.

"I refuse to give that man any power over me ever again. He has already destroyed my entire life once, and there's nothing he can do to me that he hasn't already done. I won't let him instill fear in me or take away the newfound courage I've found in myself. I won't allow his presence to affect my life again."

We sat there in silence for a few moments, the words and memories circling the air around us, before he spoke, his intense eyes never leaving mine.

"I will never truly know what you went through or how you survived what you did. We are all in awe of you. The complete strength of will you show is astounding. But there is something I do need to say and I need you to remember. You are not alone anymore and you never will be again. Ask any one of us and we will all tell you the same thing."

Nothing I had said since waking up affected me as much as him saying those words to me with that amount of conviction. My heart squeezed in my chest as he kept watching me before I dipped my head slightly to acknowledge his words.

He stood in a smooth motion and made his way towards the door, leaving me to my thoughts and my morning routines.

―――――――

Entering the gym later that day to do my normal workout, I almost tripped as I walked across the threshold.

On my tongue.

The sound of flesh hitting flesh echoed through the gym as Colt and Gabe moved around the mats, their bare feet making soft slapping sounds against the rubber surface. Sweat glistened on their skin under the bright lights, giving them a slick, almost otherworldly appearance. I'd never seen them truly spar before, always leaving before they started, but now

I'm transfixed by the way their muscles flexed and rippled with each movement.

All they were wearing was shorts and skin. And the slight gleam of sweat tells me they had been there for a little while already.

I felt my cheeks heat up at the way they move around each other and I stood there just in the door watching them as they tried to land strikes on each other as they moved barefoot around the mats. It was impossible to look away.

It was like watching porn.

Gabe's eyes flickered to me in the doorway, offering Colt the distraction he needed to take him to the ground and into a hold that had Gabe tapping out in seconds. Colt released him again and they slowly returned to their feet as Gabe grouched at him about being unfairly disadvantaged.

Colt just ignored him as his eyes ran down my body taking in the gym clothes I'm wearing. He signaled for me to come to where he was standing at the center of the mats. "Come over here, princess, so I can give you a lesson on self-defense," Colt said.

I raised an eyebrow at him and smiled slightly. "Self-defense?"

"Yes, I want you to have at least the basics, just in case something happens and we're not around or occupied with other intruders," he explained.

I shrugged at that and started making my way towards him, putting my towel and water bottle on the ground at the edge of the space. I removed my shoes and socks and put them into a cubby hole near the door, returning barefoot to the mats like him.

"Let Gabe tape up your hands so you don't get hurt," Colt advised.

Gabe, who had left the mats only a moment before, returned with a roll of hand tape and motioned for me to hold out my hands. I did as instructed and he got to work wrapping up my hands and knuckles securely, his eyes flicking up to mine every now and then as he did. When he finished, he tapped the top of my hands and gave me a sharp smirk before walking away, tossing the roll back onto a bench before he took up position leaning against the wall near the door. He was still only in a pair of shorts and nothing else, and I could see his sleek muscles ripple as he crossed his arms across his chest.

I focused back on Colt to see heated amusement on his face as he watched me watch Gabe. My eyes briefly took him in again as I moved to stand before him. Where Gabe was all sleek and speed, Colt was pure power. And like Gabe, Colt still hadn't put a fucking shirt on.

Fuck me. This was going to be torture. My heart was pounding so hard I could feel it in my ears, and I was not sure if it was from nerves or arousal.

Colt waited until I appeared ready before explaining. "We'll start simple. When I come at you I want you to use both arms to knock mine outwards, and then use my momentum to grab my neck and pull down while you lift your knee up. Are you following? We will go slowly the first time. Don't actually hit my face."

I heard Gabe give a snort behind me. "Yes, don't damage his pretty boy face, he needs that to keep making you all hot and bothered."

I almost shot a look at him over my shoulder but at that same moment Colt moved towards me. He was true to his word and moved slowly, taking me through what he was trying to teach me each step, the next time he sped it up but always quickly moving his hands to grab my leg before it could chance making contact with him.

I nodded along with his instructions and followed everything he directed at me as he took me through a few different moves and techniques over the course of half an hour.

"Ok, this time I'm not telling you what to do. I'm going to come at you at normal speed and I want to see you react naturally to see how much you've learned."

He moved towards me again at a faster pace, he said he was going to do that so it didn't shock me, but I could tell he was still restraining himself and going slower than he could. He had demonstrated his true speed when I watched him with Gabe earlier.

Instead of moving how he taught me I moved to the left at the last moment, shoving both his arms towards the right and causing his momentum to twist his body in the same direction. I used my right foot to give a hard kick to the back of his right knee, collapsing that leg beneath him. His knee hit the mat hard and he grunted in surprise. I wrapped an arm around his neck from behind and used my other arm to strengthen the hold and then using that leverage I wrapped my legs around his body and fell backwards onto the mat, bringing his weight down and to the right so it didn't crush me, tucking my face into the back of his neck. He tried to move me but at that point I was locked around his body. He grunted again and tapped against my arm in the universal symbol of submission.

I released him and we both rolled in opposite directions, moving quickly to our feet to face each other.

I flashed him a broad smile as he massaged his neck and winced, then proceeded to stretch it from one side to the other.

"Kacey neglected to tell me everything obviously."

Chapter 16

Alexis

I laughed at his comment, giving a shrug of my shoulders and a slight shake of my head. "Kacey didn't really pay that much attention, especially not after Nick went to prison."

He chuckled and nodded while he moved back towards the center of the mats, changing his stance into a more professional fight position, raising his hands in a beckoning motion and said, "Okay then, Princess, you have my attention. Show me what you've got."

I felt the need to even the playing field even slightly. After spending so long in close contact with him shirtless it was only fair, and at that point I was starting to get really hot. I was going to blame the exercise and not that he had me hot and bothered as Gabe suggested earlier.

Grabbing the bottom of the shirt I wore, I pulled it off over my head, leaving me in just my sports bra and leggings. I heard a choking sound before Gabe started coughing and I looked over to see that he had been taking a drink of water when I had decided to take off my shirt. Oops.

I laughed and threw the shirt in his direction while he shot me a hot, viscous look. The distraction was enough that I missed Colts reaction and by the time I focused back on him his face was a careful mask again.

I moved back onto the mat into position in front of him as I shook my arms back out at my sides, prepared to have a better challenge now that the proverbial gloves were off. Bringing my hands back up to a loose ready position I took slow, deliberate steps, circling him as he expertly mirrored my movements. I could sense his unwavering focus on me, as if he was waiting for me to make a mistake. I could tell he wouldn't make the first move, he was waiting for me and obviously had the patience of a saint.

I moved to leap at him and he saw the motion and moved to intercept me. I dropped at the last moment, kicking out at his leg yet again, causing him to stumble, but not go down. In a split second, he pivoted and wrapped his muscular arm around my neck, lifting me up effortlessly. The suddenness of the move caught me off guard, but I managed to stay alert. I twisted and jabbed my elbow back, connecting with his jaw and he released me instantly, moving away as he rubbed a hand along where I connected. I could still see the amusement plastered across his face and he chuckled softly.

With a fierce determination, he lunged at me and we engaged in a fierce sparring session. We traded strikes and blocks with an intensity that left us both breathless and hot. After twenty grueling minutes, I gathered all my strength and aimed a powerful roundhouse kick at his face, his hand only snapped out to stop it at the very last moment, he held my foot and tutted at me. Using the hold he had on my foot he swept my other leg from under me, sending me crashing to the mats, my back slapped against the foam. I went to roll away but he was already on me, straddling my hips and using his feet to hold my legs down while he grabbed both of my wrists to hold above my head, the move bringing his face closer to mine. His hold is strong and I could barely move any of my body.

"Enough," he rasped at me as I tried to break his hold on me, stilling my movements and bringing my focus back to him.

The heat in his gaze was enough to set me on fire beneath him as he dropped his body down further against mine, letting me feel his solid erection only inches away from where I desperately wanted it.

I was panting beneath him from the workout we had already put each other through only to then have my body wanting a completely different kind of workout with him. I arched my back slightly, causing my breasts to press against his chest, eliciting a noticeable reaction from him as his eyes widened and his nostrils flared.

"Fuck it," was the last thing I heard before his mouth was crashing into mine, his lips and tongue devouring me as we still battled for dominance even as we kissed. He tasted vaguely of coffee and I also smelled the faint scent of it mixed in with his normal sandalwood.

He groaned into me and released my arms and legs in order to slide his body down against mine, and I parted my legs for him automatically, allowing him to settle his covered erection against my heated core, dragging a gasp from me in response. He used that opportunity to shift his body more and started dragging his kisses slowly down my throat as he fisted my hair to pull my head backwards to give himself better access. Once he reached the hollow at the base of my throat he licked a hot line all the way back up to my mouth.

I was burning alive. He had started an inferno blazing in my body that couldn't be controlled. And I didn't want it to be.

"Do you want this?" He demanded as he moved his hips, rubbing his erection against my throbbing pussy through our clothes. His hot gravelling voice was turning the heat up even more and I felt like a wet puddle beneath him.

"Yes," I moaned as I arched and tried to use my hands on his neck to bring his mouth back to me but he resisted, using a hand beside my head to prop himself up and further away from me.

"And do you want all of us? I know they told you we are a package deal."

I couldn't stop my thoughts from drifting to that particular aspect for days, so his question was almost redundant. Still, I replied without a shred of doubt, my breath hitching in anticipation. "Yes, all of you."

But Colt wasn't convinced yet. He needed to be sure. "Once we start this, there's no going back. Are you sure you can handle all of us?" he asked, his tone cautious yet intense.

My answer was immediate and unwavering. "God, yes." My heart was racing with excitement and my body was thrumming with desire. I was all fucking in.

He chuckled at my response, but there was a hint of challenge in his voice. "We'll certainly see, won't we?"

The pressure of his thumb against my jaw moved my head to the side and I was suddenly looking into heated blue eyes as Gabe watched us intently from where he stood leaning against the wall.

"Is he staying or leaving?" Colt asked, his breath hot against my cheek as he moved his face closer to mine again.

"Staying," I panted out, my heart racing.

Gabe's eyes flared at my response while he adjusted what I could already tell is an impressive package in his pants.

Colt hummed approvingly in my ear as he too turned briefly to look at Gabe, his own cheek almost brushed against mine.

"He won't be joining us this time. He lost our sparring session, and we had a wager on it, but I'm willing to use this opportunity to clear that debt. He's going to stay over there and watch. But don't you worry about him, princess, he very much likes to watch... we all do."

Umm, yeah I had already gotten that impression. Gabe's lips were parted on a slight pant as he rubbed the heel of his palm against his cock through the material of his shorts.

As I watched Gabe, Colt took advantage of the distraction and flicked his tongue at my ear lobe before biting down on it, eliciting a gasp from me. Gabe groaned and shifted his hand to squeeze himself instead of continuing to rub.

Colt shifted his kneeling position to free his hands, and then trailed them slowly down my body, starting from my collarbone and ending at my hips. With no hesitation, his fingers and thumbs traced over the visible scars that he came across. He then moved his hands in a return journey, back up my body until they reached my sports bra. Holding my gaze, he slowly lowered the zipper at the front of the bra, and I felt each individual prong of the zipper as it parted for him. The heat in my body rose with each tiny movement, and as soon as my breasts were exposed to the air, his hands quickly replaced the fabric. He kneaded the soft flesh under his palms, moving the weight of them around while thumbing over my hard nipples. Then, he took my nipples in his fingers and squeezed, eliciting another moan from me as I arched my back beneath him, pushing my breasts further into his hands.

"Mmmm, so fucking responsive," he rasped before lowering his face and drawing one of my nipples into his hot mouth while his hand continued playing with the other. His tongue circled around the hard peak several times before he took it between his teeth and bit down.

A loud, guttural moan escaped my lips, and I couldn't help but cry out, "Fuuuuck," as the pleasure overwhelmed me. I bit down hard on my wrist, trying to stifle the obscene sound.

Colt quickly grabbed my arm, pulling it away from my face. "No, no, no," he said firmly. "I want to hear you, princess. I want you screaming my name so loud that the whole house knows exactly what we're doing in this room." His eyes locked onto mine as he spoke, the intensity of his gaze sending shivers down my spine.

I had thought, especially after the night before, that Hunt would be the first one to have sex with me. But after hearing that from Colt's mouth I vowed to myself that if I didn't get his cock inside me in the next ten minutes I would scream, and not the way he wanted me to.

It's as if he could read my thoughts, and he growled, his voice low and dangerous. "I know you haven't had sex with any of the others yet, and maybe starting with me isn't the wisest choice, but I can't stop now. I'm not gentle, and I won't be gentle. Both Gabe and I prefer it rough, so if you're looking for sunshine and sweetness and fun, then Hunt is your best bet." The words leave his mouth in a dark, sultry tone that makes my body quiver with need.

At that moment, I couldn't care less about anything else, but the question slipped out anyway. "What about Rome?" I asked, my voice barely a whisper.

Colt grinned at me, his hand trailing back down my body again. "Rome is a whole other beast," he said with a knowing glint in his eye. "I know you've already taken a peek at him. He has his own unique kinks that I'm sure you'll become familiar with in no time at all."

My body shuddered at the thought and the memory, and I couldn't help but let out a soft moan. Yes, I was totally here for that.

His hand boldly slid into my pants, his eyes widened in surprise when he found no further barriers, his fingers gliding straight through my wet folds. I let out a breathless gasp at the sensation, my body responding eagerly to his touch.

He tilted his head at me, licking his bottom lip as he glanced down between my legs. "Hmmmm, where is your underwear, princess?" he asked, a hint of amusement in his voice.

Without waiting for a response, Colt thrust two of his fingers into me, his thumb finding and circling my clit. The sudden sensation caused my back to arch again and my moans grew louder, pleasure pulsing through my body.

Colt groaned, his eyes molten with desire, as he continued to thrust into me with his fingers. "I think she came down here looking to get fucked, don't you, Gabe?" he asked, a smirk playing at the corner of his lips.

"Abso-fucking-lutely," Gabe responded huskily.

My eyes flicked over to Gabe, his hand had slid into his own pants as he watched us. The sight of his hand matching the movement of the fingers inside me only added to the pleasure coursing through my body.

Colt recaptured my attention as he pulled his fingers out of my pants and sucked them into his mouth, moaning at the taste of me. His eyes darkened with desire as he spoke, his words raw and carnal. "You taste so fucking good. I want to spread you open and feast on your pussy until you drown me, but I don't have the patience today. The first time I make you come, I want to feel you strangling my cock."

The controlled and polite Colt was gone, replaced by a primal and hungry man who looked like he wanted to devour me whole and dirty talk his way between each bite.

And god, did I want to be devoured by him.

Chapter 17

Alexis

With a firm grip on the sides of my leggings, he pulled them down, the fabric clinging to my skin for a moment before they slid off my legs and flew behind him. His eyes were fixated on me as he stood up, yanking his own shorts down and off his legs, carelessly tossing them away. He dropped back down between my legs, his gaze burning with desire as he repositioned himself.

As I caught a glimpse of his cock, doubt began to creep into my mind. He was far from small and definitely larger than any man I had ever been with before. But despite the momentary hesitation, I still wanted him inside me desperately.

Colt's hand wrapped around his cock as he rubbed the head against my slick pussy, spreading my wetness all over himself. "Last chance, princess," he said, his eyes locked onto mine. "If you don't want this, if you don't want us, speak now."

As I stole another glance at Gabe standing by the door, I noticed he too had discarded his pants. My eyes were immediately drawn to the glint of metal at the head of his cock - it was pierced, just as I had imagined when we kissed. The sight made me emit a low growl, as I became increasingly impatient. "Enough with the teasing, give me your fucking cock already Colt or I'll tell Gabe to take your place."

The thrust of him inside me shouldn't have taken me by surprise, but it did, the sudden stretch of him caught me off guard. The pain captured my breath in my lungs and caused tears to well up in my eyes. Even though I knew he was big, the reality of it is almost overwhelming. And yet, I could tell that he wasn't even fully inside me yet. I whimpered in response, but despite his earlier talk of roughness, he gave me a moment to adjust before pulling back and thrusting again. I could feel every thick hard inch of him as he thrust inside of me. As he sank deeper into me, I could feel my body starting to relax and open up to him, allowing him to bury himself to the hilt. His pubic bone ground against my already sensitive clit, sending a jolt of pleasure through me despite the discomfort.

As he groaned, I could feel the vibration of his voice through his chest, adding another layer of stimulation to the overwhelming sensation. "Fuck," he moaned, "your pussy feels like heaven. You're so fucking hot and wet and tight." The steady stream of filth from his mouth was almost enough to push me over the edge, without any further stimulation.

He withdrew and then plunged back into me with a force that made my breasts bounce and my hands scrambled for a grip on the slippery surface of the mats. The sound of skin slapping against skin filled the room, punctuated by our gasps and moans.

He hooked his arms under my knees, using a tight grip on my waist to lift my lower body up with his as he straightened his hips. My body weight rested on my shoulders, still pressed against the mats. The shift in position made me gasp, and I felt his next thrust hit me at an even deeper angle. It was a sensation I had never experienced before, and it sent a jolt of pleasure straight through my body.

My hands frantically searched for something to grip onto and finally found the edge of the mats. I held on tight as Colt started to thrust into me with more speed and force. The sound of our skin slapping together echoed through the room, along with my own moans and cries.

Each thrust sent shockwaves of pleasure through my body, making me moan uncontrollably. His hips collided with mine with a sharp sound, and I felt the orgasm building rapidly inside me, making me clench tightly around his thick cock. The sensations were overwhelming, and I felt my body tensing up, ready to explode in pleasure.

"Cum for me princess. Cum all over my cock like a good girl."

Colt's dirty talk echoed in my mind as my body exploded. I threw my head back and let out a loud moan as my orgasm crashed over me like a wave. The intense sensation sent shockwaves through my body, making my back arch and my toes curl. I felt Colt's grip tighten on me as my inner walls clenched around him. He slowed down his movements, prolonging the pleasure coursing through my body.

"God, you feel amazing," Colt growled, his voice thick with desire. "You're squeezing my cock so fucking good, princess. You're such a good girl, aren't you?"

I let out a small, desperate whimper as he withdrew himself from inside me, leaving me feeling empty and longing for more. Suddenly, he flipped my body over effortlessly, positioning me on all fours in front of him. With rough hands he parted my legs wider, gripping my ass and positioning it exactly where he wanted it. With a single fluid movement, he thrust back inside me, and the unmistakable sound of his hips colliding with my ass echoed through the room. The lewd noise only served to intensify my arousal, sending a rush of heat through my body as he continued to move inside me.

Releasing his grip on one of my hips, he wrapped his hand around my ponytail, yanking my head back towards him, causing my body to arch as far back as it could. The sharp, intense pain mixed with pleasure caused me to gush and clamp down tightly around his cock as he pounded into me at a punishing pace.

"Once more, princess, and then I'll give you my cum, I'll fill up that pretty pussy of yours until you're dripping with me." His dirty words sent shivers down my spine, propelling me towards the brink of ecstasy. I moaned in response, the mere sound of his voice pushing me closer to the edge.

My eyes had fluttered shut in anticipation, but a hand at my jaw jolted me back to reality. The firm grip forced me to reopen my eyes, which had been closed without me even realizing it. The thumb and finger squeezed my cheeks to push my face back even further, causing my neck to strain.

Gabe stood before me, his cock pulsing in his hand as he demanded, "Tongue out, and don't you dare spill a drop. And don't fucking swallow until we tell you to."

Without hesitation, I stuck out my tongue, feeling the head of his cock almost resting against it. Gabe's hand moved up and down his length, and I used the tip of my tongue to flick the piercing on the head of his cock. He gasped in surprise, not expecting such an immediate response, before he let out a deep, guttural moan.

The first burst of his hot cum landed on my tongue precisely where he wanted it, and I struggled to resist the urge to swallow him whole. The salty taste of his release lingered on my tongue as he continued to pump his hips, making sure I received every last drop.

After he was done, Gabe dropped to his knees in front of me, his face close to mine as I obediently stuck out my tongue for his inspection. His cum is still lingering in my mouth as he glanced behind me at the man who was still thrusting slowly into me, giving a slight nod of approval before refocusing on my face. "Swallow," he ordered, his voice firm and commanding.

Without hesitation, I let his salty taste slide down my throat. When I finished, I opened my mouth to show him that I had done as he instructed.

"Good fucking girl," he praised, before his lips collided with mine in a rough, consuming kiss. His tongue thrust into my mouth, eagerly seeking and tangling with mine, as if he was savoring the taste of himself on my lips. Our moans melded together as our tongues entwined, and I felt the cool metal of his piercing pressing against my tongue, intensifying the sensation.

I felt his hand move down my body, his fingers found one of my nipples and gave it a sharp, almost painful twist that shot pure fire in a line straight to my pussy, causing Colt to grunt behind me and pick up his rough pace once again.

Each thrust sent shockwaves of pleasure through my body, making me moan uncontrollably. His hips collided with mine with a sharp sound, the slap of our skin together became a wild soundtrack to the almost animalistic sounds that came from us. I felt the orgasm building rapidly inside me again, making me clench tightly around his cock. The sensations were overwhelming, and I felt my body tensing up, right on the edge of a cliff.

Gabe released my mouth and moved back enough to watch my face just as his exploring fingers found my overly sensitive clit. He used my own wetness to make circular motions around it a few times before he took it between his fingers and gave it a firm pinch.

Holy. Fuck.

An explosion of stars filled my vision as my orgasm tore through me, launching me out of this world. Thankfully, there were no neighbors within miles because the scream that escaped my lips would have undoubtedly led them to report a potential murder to the police. In all honesty, I was surprised that the windows of the house hadn't shattered, but I couldn't check at that moment, nor for the next hundred years, because I was pretty sure I had died. I had never experienced such an intense orgasm before.

If there had been any lingering doubts about whether the other two occupants of the house were aware of what was happening, they were totally utterly gone.

The loud shout and deep moan from behind me was the only warning that Colt reached his climax before I felt him erupt inside me. I could feel his heat flood me as his pace stuttered and slowed, his panting breath loud now that my cries had reduced to soft whimpers.

Another groan escaped Colt's lips as he slowly pulled out of my body, and his fingers continued to clench tightly onto my hips, leaving behind a trail of finger marks.

I felt a warm gush of fluid as our mingled releases began to trickle down my thighs. Colt released his hold on my hip with one hand and used his fingers to capture our sticky mixture before plunging them back into my sensitive pussy, as if determined to keep his cum inside me. I attempted to glance back at him over my shoulder, only to find that his intense gaze was fixated entirely on my pussy and the path his fingers were taking through our mess.

Then, he looked up and beyond me to Gabe before holding his wet fingers out across my body. Gabe leaned over me and took Colt's fingers into his mouth, using his tongue to savor the taste of our combined cum.

Fuck.

If I wasn't so thoroughly exhausted, the sensations coursing through my body at that sight would have had me begging for more, and the pulsing heat emanating from my pussy tried to lure me into pushing past my fatigue. However, the creeping haziness at the edge of my mind signaled that it was time to rest.

As Colt released his hold on my other hip, I collapsed forward onto the mats, and Gabe rolled me gently onto my back, tenderly moving my sweat-soaked hair out of my face. I was only vaguely aware of Colt returning from the bathroom with a damp cloth and carefully cleaning me up while Gabe breathed into my ear about how much of a good girl I was for them, making me take sips of my water.

Chapter 18

Alexis

I must have passed out, and I was unsure of how long I'd been asleep before I gradually became aware of my surroundings. I found myself tucked into my bed with Gabe, who was fast asleep with his arms tightly wrapped around my stomach and breasts, snoring softly with his face nuzzled into my neck. The dim light through the window suggested that it was already late in the evening, indicating that I've been asleep for quite some time. Someone had already turned my closet light on so I didn't wake to darkness.

As I became more conscious, the urge to pee took over, and I tried to slide out of Gabe's embrace as gently as possible, but he clung on to me tightly. So, I resorted to running my finger along his arm repeatedly until he twitched and rolled over on his back, spreading himself out on the bed like a starfish.

If I weren't so desperate to relieve myself, I would have taken a moment to admire how adorable and sexy he looked. And to realize that we were both still naked.

Instead, I slipped out of bed and hurried into my ensuite, turning on the bright light and closing the door for some privacy. After relieving myself and washing my hands, I glanced at my reflection in the mirror. My hair was a wild mess, my lips were swollen and darker than usual, and I could already see bruises starting to form on various parts of my body from Colt and Gabe's rough attention.

After taking out my hair tie and quickly brushing it, I decided it was good enough and turned to head back to bed. But when I opened the door, I saw Gabe leaning against the bathroom doorway. Without hesitation, he lifted me up and over his shoulder, giving my ass a sharp slap when I tried to resist.

I let out a moan as his hand soothed the sting and sent a pulsating wave of heat through me. He placed me gently on the bathroom counter and chuckled at my flushed face, "Rome's going to have so much fun with you, and I hope he lets me watch."

Despite my protests, Gabe paid no attention and proceeded to open the shower door, turning on the water and testing the temperature before coming back to retrieve me. Once I'm under the water, he set me down on my feet but didn't leave my side, closing the shower door behind us. Luckily, the shower was spacious enough to accommodate a party. Gabe then took his time to wash me thoroughly, including shampooing and conditioning my hair, being mindful of the sensitive areas of my body. The experience felt like pure bliss.

Gabe gave me one last sweep with the washcloth before discarding it onto the shower floor. He then used his warm, bare hands to gently cup and squeeze my breasts, causing my body to moan with pleasure. Next, he lowered his head and wrapped his lips around my sensitive nipple, flicking the metal stud in his tongue across the peak while he licked and sucked on it. The sensation was almost too intense, causing me to gasp and arch my back, pushing my breast deeper into his mouth.

"Your moans have been driving me wild ever since I started washing your beautiful body," he said, causing me to flush in embarrassment. I had been so caught up in the pleasure of his touch that I hadn't even realized I was making any noise.

Before I could apologize, Gabe's mouth crashed onto mine, cutting me off. He reached down with both hands and lifted me up, pressing me against the wall of the shower. I wrapped my arms and legs around him, feeling his hard body against mine and his cock trapped between us. With one arm still around his neck, I used my free hand to slide down and grasped his length, flicking my thumb over his piercing. The deep, rumbling groan that escaped him in response sent another wave of need pulsing through my body.

"How sore are you?" he asked, his voice rough with desire.

I took a moment to assess my body, knowing that I had no objection to swallowing his cum again if I was too sore. However, I felt only a slight tenderness, so I responded with a breathless plea, "Fuck me, Gabe. Make me scream for you."

He responded with a pained moan and withdrew his cock from my grasp, only to plunge it deep inside me with a single motion. A wild noise escaped me, almost animalistic. He may not have been as thick and long as Colt, but the curve of his cock and the angle of his thrust caused his piercing to make direct contact with my G-spot, sending intense waves of pleasure through me.

After checking to make sure I was okay, Gabe didn't hold back. Despite not being too sore after taking Colt, the force of Gabe's thrusts pushed me towards the tender edge. I bounced against the wall, feeling bruised from the harsh treatment, but my body's response told a different story, it seemed to enjoy the mix of pain and pleasure.

The sounds we made become increasingly primal, echoing around the small bathroom. The intensity of our pleasure turned us both on even more, evident in the way Gabe pounded into me with force.

As my legs started to slip down from around Gabe's body, he hooked one of his arms under my leg to hold it up while the other leg barely touched the shower floor. Taking advantage of the shift in position, he twisted my body sideways, and I felt him hitting new places inside me. He slid a hand up to grasp the front of my throat, exerting gentle pressure that sent a jolt of desire through me.

His movements became erratic as my body started to tense and spasm around him, causing him to falter in his pace and let out a deep, gravelly moan. Leaning forward, he flicked his tongue against the edge of my mouth as he breathed heavily against my face, tightening his grip on my throat and cutting off my air.

I felt the heat building up inside me as he urged me on, his voice rough with desire. "That's it, beautiful, cum for me. Squeeze my dick with that hot fucking pussy of yours," he growled.

As his hand released my throat, I gasped for air and exploded into a mind-blowing orgasm. My loud cries echoed off the shower walls. He slammed his hand against the wall and bit into the flesh between my neck and shoulder, causing me to writhe in pain and pleasure. Another smaller pulsing orgasm rippled through me as he moaned low in my ear and emptied himself deep inside me.

As he slowed to a stop, he licked his way up from where he bit all the way to my lips, thrusting his tongue into my mouth in an imitation of what his cock was just doing to my pussy. The taste of my own blood on his lips made me realize that he broke the skin of my shoulder with his teeth, leaving another bruise to add to the collection.

He set me down slowly and proceeded to wash me thoroughly again, humming happily under his breath while I became a languid, pliable doll in his hands.

After he thoroughly washed me again, he pulled me out of the shower and wrapped a fluffy white towel around me, drying me off gently. He then led me back to the bedroom, where he tucked me back into bed and curled up behind me like a monkey, his breath hot against my neck.

"Sleep," he whispered, his voice lulling me back into a drowsy state. Although I wanted to protest, the warmth of his embrace and the exhaustion from our activities was too much to resist. My mind drifted off into a deep, peaceful slumber.

Chapter 19

Colt

Even though I was with Lexi only hours before, the sounds of Gabe and Lexi together in the shower had me retreating to my own cold shower in an attempt to take the edge off the fire inside me again.

It didn't work.

The memory of her body coming apart under me, and the feeling of her tight pussy gripping my cock, was still fresh in my mind.

Trying to distract myself from these thoughts, I ducked my head under the cold water and placed a hand on the tiles for support. However, the cool water only heightened my arousal, so I turned up the heat as I wrapped my other hand around my cock and began to stroke myself.

Moving my hand along my length, I moaned softly. I sped up my strokes, the image of Lexi's glistening pussy engulfing my cock firmly etched in my mind, and I imagined it was her instead of my own hand.

I pumped my hand faster, my breaths coming out in short gasps as I felt the tension building in my body.

My mind was flooded with memories of the way her skin felt against mine, the way she tasted, and the way she smelled. I was consumed with the desire to feel her wrapped around me again. I pictured her writhing beneath me, moaning my name as I explored every inch of her body.

I could feel myself getting closer, my breaths quickening and my heart racing.

I pressed my forehead against the cool tiles, my hand moving at a frenzied pace as I approached my release.

My muscles tensed as the pleasure washed over me, the memory of Lexi's body driving me over the edge. I bit down on my lip to keep from moaning too loudly, my hand never faltering as I rode out my orgasm and hot waves of my cum hit the shower wall.

Afterwards, I leaned heavily against the tiles, the hot water pounding against my back. My breathing slowly returned to normal as I tried to calm my racing heart.

With a sigh, I turned off the water and stepped out of the shower, my body still humming with residual pleasure. I used the towel to dry myself off before I wrapped it around my hips and moved back into my bedroom.

My stride remained steady as I walked towards my closet, even though I noticed the slight movement from the armchair in the corner of my room. Through the dim light, I could just make out Rome sitting there, watching me intently. It's not like we hadn't been through a lot together, so I was not even mildly embarrassed that he just heard me getting off with my own hand.

Honestly, it wouldn't be the first time and I doubted it would be the last.

As I finished dressing, Rome's serious expression caught my attention. I raised an eyebrow in question, silently asking him what was on his mind. After a moment of contemplation, he took a deep breath and spoke up.

"Kacey is Lexi's ex," Rome revealed.

I faltered, caught off guard. "What do you mean?" I asked.

"I found some information that suggests they had a sexual relationship in the past. It seems like it ended around the time of the trial, but they definitely have a history," he clarified.

"What kind of information did you find?" I asked.

Rome hesitated before replying. "Just some texts. There aren't any images or public outings to prove anything given her position in Witsec, but the texts were enough to piece it together."

I sat down heavily at the end of my bed, taking in this new information. Mixed emotions swirled inside me. The most prominent being the tinge of guilt that I am now involved with my friend's ex.

However, I reminded myself that we are all adults and there was no true betrayal. In the end, it was up to Lexi to decide what made her happy.

"I had a feeling there was more to that call," I said, musing to myself. "It seemed odd that he'd cash in that favor for something like this."

Rome nodded in agreement. "Yeah, it definitely caught me off guard."

I considered his words for a moment before I spoke up again. "Are you sure it's over between them? Did the texts give any indication of a reason?"

Rome shook his head. "No, there wasn't anything specific. They just stopped talking outside of what was necessary during the trial."

I released a heavy sigh, feeling a weight of responsibility settle on my shoulders. "I'll need to have a conversation with Lexi to see if there's anything we should be concerned about, probably not straight away, but soon," I said, as I considered the potential ramifications of our recent actions. "But I don't believe it will change anything. We've already gone too far down this road."

He grinned devilishly, a mischievous twinkle in his eye. "Oh, I heard," he teased, his tone suggestive, causing me to roll my eyes and groan as the memory of her resurfaces.

Suddenly, he broke the silence with an unexpected question, his tone serious and earnest. "So, no regrets?" he asked, his gaze fixed on mine, searching for any hint of hesitation or remorse.

I couldn't help but laugh at his question. "Absolutely fucking not," I replied, my tone confident and unapologetic. "Like Hunt said, pure fucking sin, and I will happily be a sinner after today."

Despite Rome's grin, I couldn't help but feel a knot in my stomach as I asked the dreaded question. "Anything on Dominick?" I knew that his presence posed a significant risk to Lexi, and the lack of progress in finding him was unsettling.

As expected, Rome's expression darkened. "Still nothing. And I'm trying everything," he responded, frustration clear in his voice.

"We might need to consider reaching out to some of our more shadowy contacts," I suggested, the gravity of the situation weighing heavily on me. It was a risky move, but one that may be necessary if we wanted to bring Dominick to justice and ensure Lexi's safety.

Rome nodded in agreement, but I could tell that the thought of involving our more unsavory acquaintances doesn't sit well with him. We both knew that the road ahead would be difficult and dangerous, but we were willing to do whatever it took to protect those we cared about.

And I did care about her. More than I should after such a short period of time.

Although I knew that part of our conversation had come to an end, Rome remained deep in thought in the armchair. I gave him some space to gather his thoughts before he spoke up again.

He looked at me with a worried look in his eyes. "Do you think she'll be okay with me and what I like?" he asked tentatively.

I gave him a reassuring smile. "The only way to find out is to try," I replied, hoping to ease his concern. "And if it helps, I did hint at your tastes with her earlier."

He leaned forward, intrigued. "How did she react?" he asked.

A grin spread across my face as I recalled the memory. "Let's just say, you should have heard her moan," I replied, with a hint of mischief. "But like I said, just be careful."

He cocked his head, considering my words. "With her body? Or my heart?" he asked, his voice laced with concern.

"Both," I answered firmly.

He looked down, lost in thought for a moment before admitting, "It might already be too late."

I nodded in understanding. We were both in this together, with our own fears and doubts to overcome.

"I know I was the one who told you to get out of your own way," Rome said with a rueful smile. "I guess I can't take my own advice."

He left me to my own thoughts again, sliding silently from the room and closing the door behind him.

Chapter 20

Alexis

I had come to the conclusion that exercising and running were great for my body.

The sexual acrobatics that I had put it through the day before? Not so much.

As I woke up, I felt an intense soreness in parts of my body that I hadn't even known could ache. I attempted to bury my face even deeper into the softness of the pillows in a futile effort to disappear from my discomfort.

A half-suppressed chuckle from my right side made me lift my head up, blinking my still-sleepy eyes. There was Hunt, lying on his side facing me, with his head propped up on his hand, a mischievous grin on his face. On the other side of me, Gabe grumbled incoherently as he shifted closer under the sheets.

"Do you know how you're feeling right now?" Hunt asked, still wearing his cheeky grin. "Do you want to know what's good for that? Definitely not sex."

I let out a groan of irritation and shoved him playfully in the chest, causing him to topple off the side of the bed with a laugh.

He popped his head up from the side of the bed and rested it on his folded arms, donning an obviously fake stern expression. "On a serious note, the sound of you cumming will forever live rent free in my mind. It was so fucking hot. In fact, I think Rome might have recorded some of it if you want to hear it for yourself."

I let out another groan and let my head fall back onto the bed. "Please stop talking."

He chuckled in response. "Oh, come on, sweetheart."

I pointed towards the door. "Get out!"

I heard him stand up, still laughing loudly. "Would you like me to help massage your sore muscles?" he offered.

A pillow was thrown over me, and I caught a glimpse of it hitting Hunt square in the face. I started giggling, which only made Hunt grumble about the unfairness of the world as he dragged his feet out of the room, making me laugh even louder.

As I turned my head towards Gabe, I found him rubbing his hands over his face in an attempt to wake up. After dropping his hands, he looked over at me and reached over to tuck a strand of my hair behind my ear, his hand gently cupping my cheek. I tilted my head into his hand, closing my eyes and inhaled deeply, taking in the scent that was all Gabe.

"How are you feeling, beautiful?" he asked.

"Well fucked" I replied with a smirk.

His snort turned into a loud laugh, causing me to grin. "You're just as bad as Hunt," he commented.

I let out a heavily exaggerated gasp, pretending to be offended.

"Joking aside, how are you coping with everything that happened yesterday?" he asked, his tone serious.

"Are you worried that I might want to run away?" I questioned in response.

He gives a small shrug, but I can see the underlying worry in his gesture. "Maybe," he admitted.

Sitting up, I looked at him seriously. It was the first time I'd seen Gabe look vulnerable, and I didn't like the fact that he felt that way.

"For starters, it's a little hard to run away when we're in a safe house for a reason," I reassured him. He grimaced, but I continued. "Secondly, I told Colt yesterday that I'm all in, and I meant it. I'm all in, Gabe."

He reached over and drew my face to his, brushing his lips softly against mine. "So are we, beautiful."

"Good. Now, out you go so I can walk like a drunk cowboy to the bathroom without the embarrassment of you watching me," I teased.

His laughter trailed after him as he exited the door, making me grin. I slid out of bed and waddled over to the bathroom with a wince.

After spending far too long under the hot shower, I finally exited my bedroom feeling almost human again. As I wandered downstairs, I spotted Colt relaxing on one of the couches with a book. I padded softly towards him, and his eyes flicked up and warmed when he saw me. He lifted an arm and motioned for me to take a seat with him and cuddle.

Who could say no to cuddling up against Colt? Certainly not me.

I snuggled into his side, and he hummed as his arm wrapped around me, pulling me even closer. "I gather from your lack of gym clothes that you're skipping your workout today," he observed.

I laughed softly. "Umm, I think I exercised enough yesterday to skip several workouts."

Colt's warm grin spread across his face, his green eyes sparkled with amusement. "Is that a complaint I hear?" he quipped, teasing me.

I couldn't help but play along. "You mispronounced 'compliment'," I retorted, grinning back at him.

He let out a hearty laugh, his hand coming up to brush a strand of hair from my face before he pressed a soft kiss to my forehead. Setting his book aside, he wrapped his now free arm around me, pulling me closer to his side. "Did you want to watch a movie or something?" he asked.

I considered his offer for a moment before replying, "Maybe. Is there the potential for snacks?"

He chuckled, giving me a playful look. "Maybe, if they are healthy snacks."

I raised an eyebrow at him, a sly smile on my lips. "I will agree to one healthy snack for every two non-healthy snacks."

Colt shook his head, chuckling again. "You're as bad as the twins," he said fondly. "Okay then, up and choose a movie, and I will go get your snacks, princess."

I rose from the couch, ready to pick a movie to watch, but before I could take more than a step, Colt smacked a hand on my ass, causing me to stumble. I shot him a look over my shoulder, but all I got in response was a cheeky grin as he wandered off to the kitchen, leaving me to recover my balance. I made my way to the collection of movies and started browsing, looking for something interesting to watch. Finally, I settled on one that I knew had probably never been watched in this house and I couldn't help but wonder who had even added it to the collection.

As I loaded up the movie and paused it, waiting for the snacks to arrive, I got comfortable on the couch again. Just then, Hunt and Gabe walked into the room. "What are we watching?" Hunt asked curiously. Gabe plopped down on the other couch and glanced at the TV screen before giving a low whistle.

Gabe smirked mischievously and suggested, "Are we trying to piss Colt off? I feel like this is your way of getting back at the boss man, and I'm happy to support you. Subtly, of course. Maybe from another room."

I couldn't help but snicker at his comment and threw a pillow at his face, which he effortlessly caught and used to prop up his head. Colt came back with the snacks and spotted the opening credits of the movie paused on the screen, shooting me a frown as he sat down next to me.

"Hey, I was all set to go with an action-packed movie with guns blazing, but then you smacked me on the ass," I teased, reaching for the snacks in Colt's arms. He reluctantly handed them over, grumbling under his breath. I swore I even heard the word 'brat' thrown in, much to my amusement.

As I was about to start the movie, Rome appeared coming down the stairs. "No gym today?" he asked.

Colt laughed, and I shot him a playful glare. Ignoring him, I turned to Rome and shook my head. "No, not feeling like it today."

He hummed and a smile tugged at his lip while Hunt snickered and added, "Wonder why that is."

I threw the other pillow at Hunt's face in frustration. "Shut it or I'll put another chick flick on after this one," I threatened.

Rome laughed this time taking a seat on my other side. "Like that's going to stop him, who do you think added those movies to the collection in the first place."

Before I could do anything, like look for another pillow to throw, Colt was moving and rearranging me until I was lying down on the lounge with my head in his lap, his fingers playing with my hair while Rome pulled my legs up and started slowly rubbing at the muscles of my legs.

I ignored anything beyond that point for obvious reasons.

Chapter 21

Alexis

While I was brewing my second coffee of the day in the kitchen, Sam suddenly entered, breaking the silence. I had briefly seen her earlier when she arrived and began her regular routine, with this being her final stop. I promptly grabbed another mug and prepared coffee for her as well, taking out the cookies that Hunt and I had baked the previous afternoon after watching a movie.

Before I could even ask her how she slept, Sam demanded, "You, miss, owe me details." My heart jumped into my throat as I froze.

It took me a moment to realize that she was talking about the tension she saw between Hunt and me during her last visit. She didn't know about me or my complicated situation.

"Tell me what is going on between you and that gorgeous man!" Sam pressed on, and I could feel myself turning red with embarrassment. I stammered out a hesitant "umm" and wished for the floor to swallow me up.

Sam misunderstood my hesitation, assuming that I was simply being coy about the juicy details of my relationship with one of my bosses. "Oh honey, I don't care that he is one of your bosses," she teased. "Those are the spiciest kinds of books. Please tell me there has been some spiciness."

I almost choked on my own tongue.

If only she knew. And not actually with who she was currently imagining.

But I kept up the facade, not wanting to ruin the moment. We took our coffee and cookies to the dining table and settled in for a gossip session. I steered the conversation away from the ticking time bomb that was my involvement with any of the men in the house, and Sam told me all about the new antics of her son.

As we chatted, Sam moved on to gossip about the latest entertainment news, something I had no clue about. But it was nice just to sit and listen to her, and I realized that if it weren't for my complicated situation, Sam and I could become good friends.

Once again she left the house on schedule with a hug and a promise she would get more details from me next time.

I stayed in the kitchen to finish cleaning up. Once I had put away the mugs and plates, I made my way back to the dining room. To my surprise, Rome was already there, typing away on his laptop. I couldn't help but admire him for a moment before he interrupted my thoughts with a grin.

"Nice diversion on the topic of your involvement with Hunt," he said.

For fuck's sake, how did he even hear that or know what we were talking about?

I gave him a skeptical look. "I'm starting to think you're the most dangerous one on the team," I said.

Rome chuckled. "Who, me? I'm just a geek," he replied with a shrug.

As I approached him, I let out a thoughtful hum. "You definitely don't fit the typical geek stereotype," I commented. His chuckle was so deep and husky that it sent a shiver down my spine. I refused to let my mind wander to other parts of my body.

With a playful smirk, he asked, "And what does a stereo-typical geek look like?"

I pretended to ponder for a moment, enjoying the teasing banter between us. "Hmmm, maybe skinny and weak, defi-nitely pale, can't get a tan locked in a coding cave," I replied with a grin.

As I traced my finger along the top of his laptop screen, his hand shot out and grabbed my wrist, pulling it away from his computer. I could feel his strength as he held onto me firmly. "Hmmm, I guess you're right, definitely can't say I'm pale or skinny," he said as he stood smoothly.

He used his grip on my wrist to guide me back against a clear section of the table. He took my hand and curled my fingers around the edge of the wood before doing the same with my other hand, holding both of them in place with his own. "What about weak? Where did you land on me being weak?" he asked.

His grip was so tight that I knew I wouldn't be able to move my hands even if I tried. He leaned in closer, his face only a few inches away from mine, and I could feel his warm breath on my lips.

"Umm..." I managed to stammer out, completely forgetting what we were talking about as his proximity made it difficult to focus on anything else.

I could see the different shades of brown and gold in his eyes from this proximity, but my gaze kept getting drawn back to his mouth, which hovered near mine. As I tried to bridge the gap between us, he matched my movements and pulled away, clicking his tongue and shaking his head slightly.

"Stay still," he commanded.

Seriously? How could I possibly stay still?

Despite my rapidly beating heart, I managed to remain immobile, panting softly. He drew closer to my face once again, double-checking that I'm not moving. Tilting his head, he paused so very close to me, his lips nearly brushed mine.

Slowly, he glided his tongue over my bottom lip, repeating the motion before he used his teeth to nibble on the edge of my lip. I could feel my lips parting wider as my breathing grew heavier.

He sucked my lip into his mouth, softly at first before intensifying the pressure and flicking his tongue against it. As he bit down more firmly with his teeth, I gasped and moaned, feeling as if he was tracing a direct line to my clit with his sucking and biting.

Running his tongue over the spot where he had just bitten me, he pulled back to examine me. "So, what do you think?" he asked.

"Sorry, what?" I responded.

He chuckled. "Do you think I'm weak?"

Pausing to think, I tilted my head slightly and a mischievous grin crept onto my face. "Hmm, what's in it for me if I agree that you're a super strong, buff man?"

He hummed thoughtfully, studying my expression

He drew his face close to mine once more, his expression serious once again. I remained motionless, knowing that I was not permitted to move no matter how lighthearted he may have seemed just moments before. He advanced until our lips were almost touching, and he breathed hotly against mine.

"Do you want to be my good girl?" he murmured.

Fuck. Why is that so hot? The mere sensation of his words brushing against my lips sent a shiver down my spine and my clit pulsed with need.

"Please," I whispered in response.

"Please what?" he inquired, raising an eyebrow at me.

Oh, fuck me.

"Please, Sir," I replied automatically, my voice breathy and submissive. It was precisely what he desired, judging by the way his eyes blazed with lust.

He hummed once more as he freed my hands, then lifted me up and placed me on the edge of the table. With one hand, he pressed down on my chest, laying me flat against the wooden surface.

"Hands above your head," he commanded. "Hold onto the other edge."

My hands obeyed his instructions before I even realized it, and I gripped the table tightly, feeling the roughness of the wood against my skin.

Slowly, he ran his hand down my body, never actually touching anything too sensitive or intimate. He trailed a finger along the top of my leggings, reminiscent of how I had traced my finger along his laptop screen earlier.

Hooking his fingers into the waistband of my leggings, he looked into my eyes once again. "Can I remove these?"

I could only manage a nod in response.

"Words, baby girl," he chided.

The new pet name sent a jolt of heat straight to my core.

"Yes, Sir," I managed to breathe out.

He nodded approvingly before using a finger on each hand to drag my leggings down and off, leaving my underwear behind.

"Since I already know darkness is a hard limit for you I'm not going to blindfold you with these, but we will discuss your limits soon," he said as he folded the leggings and draped them over the nearby chair while he grabbed another and set it in front of my legs. He took a seat in the chair and used his strong hands to push my legs wide apart before he then dragged my hips closer to the edge of the table right in front of him. My whole body heated at the thought of how I was now spread out for him like our nightly dinners.

He trailed his fingers softly over my knees. "Your hands are to stay exactly where they are. If you move your hands this stops. If you try to move your legs from where I place them this stops. Got it, baby girl?" he asked.

I nodded my head automatically and seconds later a sharp slap stung my inner thigh, making my shaky voice rush out of me. "Yes, Sir."

Another hum came from him as he smoothed his hands up the soft skin of my inner thighs. "Oh, and baby girl, if you cum without my permission, you will be punished."

Holy. Fuck.

Was I going to regret this?

He suddenly licked a long line up the skin to the left of where my underwear covers my pussy and I moaned. My head fell back and my eyes closed at the sensation.

He repeated the same movement on the other side, my mouth fell open as I panted heavily in response to the heat taking over my body. He licked another line more forcefully directly over the material of my covered pussy. I groaned and tightened my grip on the wood of the table, he hadn't even done much but he was propelling me towards a cliff faster than ever before.

He hooked a finger into the crotch of the underwear, pulling them aside to expose me to him. He inhaled as he leaned closer and he moaned before he breathed out in a husky voice, "Mmmm. you smell so good, baby girl, let's see if you taste just as good."

His tongue swept through the wetness of my pussy and I released an even louder moan than his.

He fell silent, his entire focus now on pleasing me. Slowly, deliberately, his tongue swept up, circling my clit with the tip before descending to my entrance. Each time he repeated the movement, the sensation sent electric shocks through my body. Finally, he withdrew his head and gently ran a finger through my wetness, coating it with my arousal before he brought it to his mouth to taste me again. The sight of him licking his finger was almost too much to bear.

He used that same finger to softly circle my clit, sending ripples of pleasure through me. But then he went even further, inserting it deep inside me and moving it in and out while he leaned forward to flick my clit with his tongue. I started to clench around his finger, but the next moment he withdrew it, placing it into his mouth with a hum. As I relaxed, he resumed licking and teasing my pussy, this time inserting two fingers and curling them up to quickly locate my G-spot with his long fingers. I was in ecstasy as his tongue flicked over my clit and my moans filled the room. My pussy clenched around him, causing him to fully retreat once more, leaving me whimpering in frustration that the orgasm was almost within reach before it slipped away.

He was torturing me. This was a legitimate form of torture, right?

He repeated the process twice more before I started to beg, my back arching and eyes squeezed shut, tears leaving hot tracks on the sides of my face as I shook uncontrollably. My hair stuck to my face with sweat.

"Please..." I moaned to him, and once again I received a sharp slap to my other inner thigh.

"Please, Sir, please," I tried again.

He moved his face away from my sensitive clit and blew a breath across it.

"Please what?" he asked.

"Please let me cum, Sir, please."

He hummed before starting to build my orgasm yet again. The sensation intensified, and I could feel myself getting closer and closer to the edge. Just as I was about to tumble over, he slowed down, leaving me hanging on the brink again.

I whimpered and he laughed softly before getting back to work, starting the climb once more, using his tongue and fingers to expertly pleasure me. I writhed under his touch, my body aching for release as he brought me closer and closer to the edge of pleasure. The intensity was so overwhelming that I was willing to give him or confess anything just to get him to let me cum.

"Please, Sir, please please please," I pleaded, my voice hoarse with desperation.

His hand that held my underwear shifted to pull them further away, his fingers then pressed firmly against my lower abdomen as his thumb moved in slow circles over my clit. The sensation building inside me was different this time, like the pressure felt when I needed to pee. I gasped at the unexpected feeling, my eyes widening just in time to see three sets of burning hot eyes watching us from the landing above.

As Rome found that spot inside me again, his fingers moved over it rougher this time, the pressure built to an unbearable level. I moaned and clenched down hard on his fingers, my body trembling with the intensity of my pleasure.

"Cum for me. Cum all over my face," he commanded, his voice rough with desire.

The pressure exploded at his permission. A scream ripped from my throat as I felt a rush of fluid gush from my pussy, my back arching so high it was almost painful. My pussy squeezed so tightly around his fingers that it must have been agonizing for him, but I was beyond caring. All I could think about was the waves of pleasure coursing through my body, my moans filling the room as I rode out my orgasm.

My mind slowly returned to the present, and I noticed that the twins were nowhere in sight. Only Colt remained, his gaze fixed on me.

"Good girl," Rome said, his voice deep and husky.

My response was only a weak whimper, my body still shook from the intense orgasm he just gave me.

Chapter 22

Alexis

I was in the kitchen washing my dishes from breakfast the next day when the twins barged in looking for me.

Without any preamble, Gabe declared, "We need to settle something."

Umm, somehow I didn't think this was about to go where my mind automatically went at the sight of them both moving towards me.

I tried to keep my expression neutral as I raised an eyebrow at him. "Yes, I'm having a torrid affair with your brother," I deadpanned, causing Hunt to choke on a laugh and Gabe to look bewildered.

"It's not really an affair when we're all aware of it," he responded.

Hunt chuckled again. "And it's not really torrid when we haven't had sex yet."

Gabe flicked his hand dismissively at his brother before turning his attention back to me. "We want to know who's faster," he said, his tone serious.

"I thought we just established I haven't had sex with Hunt to compare," I retorted, trying to keep the amusement out of my voice.

Gabe took a deep breath and Hunt continued to cackle at my response. Suddenly, Gabe grabbed a handful of my shirt and pulled me close to him, crushing his lips against mine. He pushed his body against mine, trapped me against the closest kitchen cabinet, and deepened the kiss until I couldn't help but moan.

After what felt like an eternity, he released me and stepped back, leaving me speechless. "Are you done being sassy now?" he asked, his voice husky.

I frowned at him, feeling both annoyed and turned on. "For starters, that was unfair," I said, pointing an accusatory finger at him. "And secondly, kissing me isn't exactly a deterrent." I grinned, unable to resist teasing him.

Gabe shook his head, a small smile tugged at the corner of his mouth. "Okay, fine. Before you go back to your full sass, we want to know who's faster with a weapon."

My smile got wider and I opened my mouth to sass some more, but before I could respond, he held up a hand and rolled his eyes. "Faster with a gun."

I let out a laugh. "Why do I feel like there is some sort of wager involved here?"

"When isn't there a wager, princess?" Colt's voice came from the doorway, where he leaned with his arms crossed.

I turned to him, grinning. "You're in on this, too?"

He flashed me a cheeky grin. "Of course."

I looked back at Gabe. "So, what's the wager?"

"Ten tasks with no complaints from anyone each of us beats." Gabe's proposal made me hesitate. These men were professionals and my odds weren't that great. Did I really want to owe thirty tasks if I lost?

As I shifted my head in thought, I spotted Rome hovering behind Colt, adding to the already intimidating lineup. Now it was forty tasks.

"Make it five tasks each and we have a deal," I said, feeling more confident about the new terms.

Gabe's grin widened, and Hunt pumped his fist in the air.

"You got your gun on you, princess?" Colt asked.

I reached into the pocket of my pants, pulling out my weapon. "Of course."

He stepped away from the wall and gestured towards the door leading to the backyard. "Come on then," he said, leading the way. We all followed Colt outside and no one commented when I took a moment to pause and feel the sunshine against my skin before rushing to catch up to him. I realized we were in the same spot where Hunt had given me a lesson on shooting last time and I noticed that someone had already set up for the challenge; five bottles were lined up in the distance, and a stopwatch had been left on the bench.

"Really? Was I that much of a sure thing?" I asked, looking at the others as they chuckled at my comment.

Gabe grinned at me. "We would have even accepted two tasks each."

I shook my head and laughed. "Silly man, I still would have done it if you had insisted on the ten."

Colt held out his hands, and I ejected the round from the chamber and removed the clip from my gun before I placed them into his palms, his fingers closed around them with a grin.

"Okay, rules are simple. Your gun will be disassembled and on the bench. At the signal, you are to assemble, fire at your bottle, disassemble, then raise your arm to signal that you're done. First will be Rome, then Gabe, Hunt, me, and then you, Princess."

He put the pieces of my gun on the bench in what I could see was the last position with the other guns already in pieces along the bench. He moved away from the bench after picking up the stopwatch, giving Rome a nod as he moved to stand beside me.

As Colt readied the timer, Rome positioned himself by the bench, adopting a composed stance with his hands clasped behind his back, poised for the challenge. "Go," Colt commanded.

In a flash, Rome swiftly assembled the gun and fired, shattering the distant bottle, then immediately disassembled the weapon and raised his hand. I'm still trying to process what happened when Colt stopped the timer. "Forty-four seconds," he declared.

Fuck.

Rome seemed content with his performance, but I wondered if he hadn't been practicing recently and could have done better. He shrugged before he returned to stand next to me, briefly brushing his fingers down my arm before crossing them over his chest to watch. "Gabe, it's your turn," Colt announced.

Gabe moved to take his place in front of his gun, assuming the same position as Rome with his hands behind his back. "Go," Colt commanded again.

I knew I was in trouble for this competition, but watching Rome and Gabe do this was incredibly sexy and worth the entry fee. Gabe looked wickedly handsome as he effortlessly completed the challenge, his hand raised before the glass even shattered again. "Forty-five seconds," Colt declared.

Gabe shot Rome a smug grin. "I almost had you."

Rome simply smiled. "To quote Mr. Toretto, 'It doesn't matter if you win by an inch or a mile, winning's winning.' And now you owe me five tasks."

Gabe shrugged and joined us, quietly taunting his brother, who winked at me before taking his place at the table. He took a breath, and at Colt's signal, moved with incredible speed. I had never seen anyone move that fast before, and I could already tell he was faster than the two men before him. As soon as he raised his hand, he turned to us with a manic grin.

"Forty-one seconds." Colt declared.

He cackled evilly as he walked back to stand with us and held his hand out for the stopwatch from Colt. "Suckers," he taunted.

Both of them just flipped him the bird with a uniformed synchronicity that spoke of many years training together.

Colt shook his head at them and took his place at the table, waiting for Hunt's signal. I didn't even realize I was holding my breath until his arm was in the air. All of these men had serious skills, but watching them in action was like witnessing magic in motion.

"Forty seconds. Asshole," Hunt declared.

Yep, he just proved another reason why he was their leader.

Colt sauntered back to me, his eyes scanning over my figure before he brushed his knuckles along my cheekbone. "Just block us out," he whispered, his voice low and husky. "We aren't even here. It's just you, your gun, and the target. Make me proud, princess." He leant in to press his lips against mine before abruptly slapping my ass so hard I stumbled forward, his dark chuckle followed me as I moved away from him. I couldn't help but agree with Hunt's assessment of him, the asshole.

My mind raced as I prepared for my turn. I shook my arms out and used the techniques I was taught to clear my mind of everything but the task in front of me. I clasped my hands together behind my back, mirroring the stance of the men before me, and focused on the gleaming glass bottle in the distance.

I heard Colt give the signal, but my mind and body were already in motion. I slid the gun parts together with practiced ease, feeling the familiar clicks as I loaded the clip and turned the safety off. I took aim at the target, my focus unwavering. As soon as I knew the bullet had left the chamber, I slid the pieces apart again and raised my arm.

Apart from the distant sound of the glass shattering, there was silence for several heartbeats. Then Hunt let out a loud woop, breaking the stillness. "What did I tell you all, so fucking hot," he exclaimed.

I turned back to the group to see four sets of eyes hot and burning into me, their expressions a mix of awe and disbelief.

I smiled and raised an eyebrow at Colt, who glanced down at the stopwatch in his hand. "Forty-three fucking seconds," he declared, a note of pride in his voice.

Gabe stood beside him, his mouth opening and closing in astonishment. "Fuck me," he muttered, his eyes still fixed on me.

I laughed at his mumbled words and gave him a grin. "I believe I've already done that," I retorted, enjoying the stunned expressions of the men around me.

Chapter 23

Alexis

After all was said and done we all owed Colt and Hunt five tasks each while Rome and Gabe owe me five tasks also. Poor Gabe ended up owing everyone, but he took it in stride with a shrug claiming it was worth it.

Colt made it clear that none of the tasks could involve any sexual content and they were left with a blank slate of potential tasks to assign to each other. At first, there was some hesitation and uncertainty as to what these tasks should entail. However, it wasn't long before some members of them began to take advantage of the newfound power dynamic that had emerged.

With the restriction on sexual tasks in place, they were able to assign tasks that ranged from the mundane to the ridiculous, with the aim of testing the limits of each other's obedience. Some tasks were relatively easy, such as fetching a drink or doing a simple chore. However, as the day wore on, the tasks became more demanding and even absurd, with some of them ordering others to perform acts that were humiliating or downright outrageous.

Despite the questionable nature of some of the tasks, those who were in positions of power reveled in their ability to make others do their bidding. They took great pleasure in bossing their "slaves" around and watching them perform their assigned tasks with utmost obedience. Meanwhile, those who were on the receiving end of these tasks found themselves powerless to resist, forced to comply with every order given to them by their dominant peers.

The next afternoon, I settled down on the couch, preparing to watch a movie, when Hunt strolled into the room, belting out a tune. "Lick me like a lollipop!" I couldn't help but chuckle at his antics as he plopped down next to me.

"Lollipop, huh?" I quipped, raising an eyebrow at him.

He grinned devilishly, waggling his eyebrows. "Popsicle? Banana? Salami? Sausage? Twig and berries? Frank and beans?"

His absurd suggestions caused me to burst out laughing, tears streamed down my face. "Is this a food-themed dirty talk now?" I asked in between chuckles.

Hunt chuckled along with me. "Food doesn't do it for you, huh?"

I shrugged, amused by his line of questioning. Hunt struck a thoughtful pose, tapping his finger against his lips before a lightbulb went off in his head.

"Let's try something different," he murmured, leaning in close to me with a deep, seductive voice. "I want to strip you completely naked and thrust my rock hard cock inside your tight little pussy so deeply that I'll cum so far inside you that it will give your birth control a run for its money."

In an instant, it was as if a switch had been flipped within me, unleashing a fiery passion that I could barely contain. I now officially called it my inferno switch.

The seconds that followed his proposal were thick with tension as we gazed into each other's eyes, but suddenly we were upon each other, tearing at each other's clothes with reckless abandon as our mouths collided.

I moaned loudly as his hands found my bare breasts, squeezing and kneading them while his fingers toyed with my nipples. I'm not even sure where my shirt and bra ended up – they could have disintegrated in flames for all I know – but it didn't matter as his mouth closed over my nipple and he shoved his hand down my leggings, his fingers thrusting inside me without hesitation.

We struggled for dominance as we kissed hungrily, biting and nipping at each other's lips. His other hand grasped my hair tightly, attempting to guide my head to the position he desired. Meanwhile, I slipped my hand down his sweat-pants, taking hold of his throbbing erection and gave it a firm squeeze before pumping it up and down.

We moved with feverish urgency, driven by unbridled lust and desire. He ripped off his shirt and kicked his pants off, while I frantically tore my own pants down my legs. The frenzy of passion consumed us completely as we pleasured each other with reckless abandon.

Suddenly, he took charge and moved us until I was strad-dling his waist, poised above his rock hard cock. With a long, low moan, I lowered myself onto him, taking in every inch of his impressive length. As it turned out, identical twins did indeed have almost identical cocks - the only difference being that Hunt wasn't pierced. But his cock was slightly fatter and longer than Gabe's, hitting my G-spot with ease.

I began to move my hips in a circular motion, savoring the sensation of him stretching and rubbing against my inner walls. Each slow rise and sudden drop elicited a moan of ecstasy from both of us. He urged me on, his voice husky with desire, "Ride me hard, sweetheart, fuck yourself with my cock."

And so I did, grinding my hips against his and taking him deep inside me. Our bodies moved in perfect harmony, lost in the heat of the moment and consumed by passion. With every powerful thrust, my skin slapped against his. I swiveled my hips once again and he pulled my mouth back to his for another intense kiss.

I continued to ride him hard as requested, rising up only to drop back down hard along his length and adding a rotation of my hips every few times. We both panted and moaned unashamedly, my breasts bouncing in his face until he reached for them with both hands, giving my nipples a sharp twist. I clenched down on his cock, causing him to groan, "Yes, just like that, sweetheart, strangle my cock."

My pace began to stutter as I felt my climax fast approaching. When Hunt reached a hand down between us and pinched my clit, it hit me like a steamroller. I cried out, my head falling back and my cries echoing around the room as I tried my best to keep riding him through my orgasm.

Hunt grunted as my pussy squeezed and pulsed around him, but he didn't cum.

He patiently waited for me to ride out my orgasm before rolling us over, and the new angle hit deeper than before. He took hold of my ankles and I silently thanked my best friend for all the yoga and pilates lessons, which allowed me to bend almost in half. As he thrust into me with incredible depth and force, his balls slapped against my skin and my moans became more intense with every stroke.

He tightened his grip on my ankles and growled out a command, "Keep those gorgeous legs spread for me."

Without hesitation, I immediately obeyed, wrapping my arms under my knees and held myself wide open. He released his hold on my ankles and leaned back slightly, slowing down to watch his cock thrust in and out of my pussy. A deep groan vibrated through his whole body as he admired the sight.

"Your pussy looks so fucking good swallowing my cock," he said, sending shivers down my spine. I clenched around him at his dirty words and he groaned again, resuming his hard and fast thrusting into my pussy. His hands grabbed a hold of each of my breasts, squeezing the flesh and pinching my nipples hard.

I couldn't contain my loud moans, surprised that no one was there to witness us. His hand glided up to envelop my throat, gradually tightening his grip with each forceful thrust of his hips and the sound of our skin slapping together. Meanwhile, his other hand ventured in the opposite direction, gliding through the slickness of our connection before encircling my clit with his fingers. As he began to vigorously rub my clit, the heel of his palm pressed down intensely on my lower abdomen.

I found myself struggling to breathe as his grip around my throat constricts, until eventually it completely cut off my air supply. The pressure built inside me became almost too much, my walls fluttering around his cock as he continued his punishing pace with the goal of destroying my pussy.

As he applied pressure on my clit, a rush of air entered my lungs, coinciding with the arrival of my climax, which hit me with the force of a freight train. My pussy contracted so forcefully that it ejects his cock completely, while my cum sprays all over him. "Yes, that's fucking hot, squirt for me, sweetheart!" he exclaimed. My body continued to contract intensely as he rammed his cock back inside me, thrusting vigorously into my tender pussy and coaxing out another, smaller orgasm at the end of the previous one. This brought him to the brink as well, and he let out a prolonged, deep groan as he cums deep inside me.

Both of us were gasping for air, as if we had just completed a marathon. He leaned forward against my slick body, careful not to crush me with his weight, still fully buried inside me. I wrapped my arms and legs around him, pulling him closer as he rested his forehead against mine, gazing into my eyes for a moment before he buried his face in my neck. I nestled my face into his hair and shut my eyes, savoring the blissful aftermath as my breaths slowly steadied. It appeared that he was as reluctant as I was to let go of our shared moment.

Unfortunately, like most instances in this house, our cuddling was cut short when I felt something falling on to us from above. My eyes flew open, and I saw Gabe leaning over the upstairs railing, looking down at us after throwing towels at us.

"Clean up your mess. I'm not sitting on that couch again unless I know I'm not sitting in my brother's cum," he remarked.

Hunt snickered, flipping Gabe off over his shoulder.

Gabe grinned wickedly at me. "This is why we fucked in the shower. It was practically self-cleaning."

I burst out laughing and buried my face in Hunt's skin, trying to conceal the flush that returned to my cheeks.

They were trying to kill me, I swear.

Chapter 24

Alexis

After climbing the stairs, I indulged in an extra long shower, savoring the feeling of the water cascading over my exhausted body. As I emerged from my ensuite and entered my bedroom, I was taken aback to find Colt standing in the stream of light from my closet that he must have turned on. He was positioned next to my bed, attired in nothing but a pair of sweatpants that accentuated his stunning physique, his damp hair indicating that he too had just finished showering.

With a small smile on my lips, I turned towards the closet to pick out some clothes to wear to bed. As I rummaged through my things, I playfully called out to Colt, "Are you my bear tonight?"

I heard him chuckle from behind me, and I turned to find him standing right behind me, his hand resting on the wardrobe door. He leaned in closer, caging me in with his arms as he brushed his lips against mine. His body wash filled my senses, a mix of freshness and sandalwood that was both calming and arousing.

"Bear, huh?" he asked with a smirk.

I returned his grin. "Yeah, like a nightmare bear. It's almost like a thunder buddy, but for my nightmares."

Colt let out a laugh before moving his hands to grip my hips, pushing me even harder against the wardrobe. "Maybe I just want to sleep next to you tonight, is that okay?" he suggested, his voice low and husky. I could feel my cheeks flush at his proximity and the way he was looking at me, making my heart race.

Was he serious? Who would say no to that?

I nodded eagerly. "Of course, that sounds great."

His smile softened as he gazed at me. "How have your nightmares been? The twins mentioned that you haven't been waking up from them for a few nights."

I shrugged, not knowing what else to say. "If I am having them, I don't remember."

He nodded in understanding. "That's good to hear."

His lips grazed the corner of my mouth as he tugged at the towel wrapped around me. The fabric slowly unraveled, slipping down to the floor, and he hummed in satisfaction as he slid his hands up my sides, brushing his thumbs over the sensitive undersides of my breasts.

His lips pressed against mine again with more firmness this time. The kiss deepened as his hands trailed up my body, directing my arms around his neck. I smiled into the kiss until he hoisted my body up and wrapped my legs around his waist, carrying me towards the bedroom and leaving my clothes forgotten on the closet floor.

"My clothes," I muttered to him.

"I need your skin against mine tonight," he replied, holding me tightly as he laid us down on the bed and pulled the sheets up to cover us.

He kept kissing me, just gentle brushes of his lips against mine, his hands sliding along my skin.

I pulled back from him briefly, "No sex."

A smile tugged at his lips and he raised an eyebrow at me.

"I think Hunt broke me." I said with a wince.

He chuckled, his laughter reverberated through the mattress. I couldn't help but let out a small laugh and swatted his chest. "I'm serious," I protested.

But his laughter was infectious, and I felt a warmth spread through me at the sound. "I believe you," he said, his amusement was evident in his voice.

I let out a scoff as I rolled my eyes. "You said he was all sunshine and sweetness and fun, but you conveniently ignored the feral animal lurking beneath the surface."

He chuckled at my description.

"Perhaps you bring it out in us," he suggested.

I gave him a skeptical look. "Are you really trying to blame me for this?"

"There's just something about you that makes us crave you, makes us want to unleash our inner beasts," he explained as he leaned in and sniffed the side of my neck.

"Did you just smell me?" I asked, unable to suppress my laughter.

He grinned mischievously at me. "Maybe."

"Well, down boy," I teased him.

As he continued to chuckle, he flipped me over and wrapped himself around me. With one arm under my head and the other around my waist, he slid a knee forward to tangle with mine, and we settled into a comfortable position.

We lay in silence for a while, but I knew he hadn't fallen asleep yet. Colt always waited until he knew I was asleep before he drifted off himself. "Colt?" I broke the silence.

He snuggled in closer to me. "Hmm?" he murmured.

"What will happen when Dominick is caught?" I asked, my voice barely above a whisper.

He fell silent for a moment. "What do you want to happen?" he finally responded. I could sense that he was just as scared to hear my answer as I was to give it.

"I don't want this to end," I whispered.

He planted a tender kiss on my skin. "Neither do we, princess," he assured me.

We lapsed into silence once again for a few moments.

"Why didn't you tell me that Kacey was your ex?" he asked, his tone devoid of anger.

My heart constricted at the question. "It didn't seem relevant, and to be honest, I hadn't even thought about it since I got here."

He hummed in response. "Was your relationship with him serious? Should I be worried?"

I considered his question for a moment. It was probably the first time I had reflected on that period of my life in a long time. "I'll admit that I used Kacey as a distraction from how messed up my life was at the time."

"Are you using us as a distraction now?" he probed.

"No! This is completely different," I insisted.

"In what way is it different?" he pressed on.

"I'm not the same person I was back then, and it never felt like this with Kacey," I explained.

"How does it feel now?" he asked.

"It feels like nothing else matters. Like I could take on the whole world as long as you're by my side," I confessed.

He hummed once more but then said in a stern voice. "Sleep."

I let out a giggle. "Shall I address you as 'Sir' like I do with Rome?"

He laughed softly. "Well, I wouldn't mind if you called me 'Sir' in certain situations, but it's not a fetish of mine."

He planted a kiss on my neck before nestling his face into it.

"Get some sleep, princess."

Chapter 25

Colt

When I opened my eyes, I was greeted with the sight of Lexi wrapped up in my arms. It was an entirely new experience for me, and I understood why the twins were so possessive about sleeping next to her every night. Her body was warm against mine, and I couldn't help but take in the sweet scent of the body wash she used the night before. It was a berry fragrance that filled my nose, but underneath that was the delicate fragrance that was uniquely hers, like wild roses.

Despite the intense need to be close to her, I didn't want to disturb her peaceful slumber. So, I slowly slid my arms away from her and gingerly slipped out of bed. Before leaving the room, I took one last glance at her sleeping form, silently hoping that my movements didn't wake her.

Even though it was early, my strict body clock, developed from my time in the military, had me awake and ready to start the day. I knew the others would either be awake or waking up shortly. After getting dressed, I made my way downstairs to prepare breakfast for myself. To my surprise, Rome was already in the kitchen, halfway through his toast.

"Mornin'," I mumbled as I made a beeline for the coffee. Even though I tried to maintain healthy eating and drinking habits, coffee was one thing I could never give up.

"Mornin'," Rome responded before returning to his breakfast.

We stood there in silence for what felt like an eternity, with him eating and me slowly waking up. I leaned back against the counter and took a sip of my coffee, feeling its warmth and energy starting to kick in. From the corner of my eye, I could see Rome assessing me as he finished off his breakfast.

"What is it?" I asked, knowing that he had something on his mind.

He narrowed his eyes at me as if trying to figure something out. "You look more relaxed, but I know you didn't have sex."

I laughed and shook my head. "I can blame Hunt for that. The asshole. But we did talk a little last night, and sleeping next to her was probably the best sleep I've had in a long time."

Now he was giving me a curious look and I wasn't too sure which part of my statement had caught his attention the most.

"You should give it a try, I know your sleeping habits, you could do with a decent night's sleep next to a beautiful woman," I teased.

Rome rolled his eyes but couldn't suppress a grin. "Oh, I plan to soon, I was more curious about what you discussed."

I took another sip of my coffee as I considered how to approach the topic. "I asked her about Kacey," I said finally.

Rome's eyebrows shot up, clearly surprised by my direct-ness. "And?"

I leaned against the counter, feeling more awake now that the caffeine was coursing through my veins. "She said he was a distraction for her during that part of her life."

Rome frowned at that, clearly disliking the idea that Lexi had ever been with someone else. "And are we just the same?" he asked quietly.

I shook my head. "No, she said that she feels completely different about us than she did with him."

Rome's eyes searched mine, as if he was trying to gauge whether I was telling the truth. I held his gaze, knowing that he trusted me implicitly.

"Then what did she say?" he asked softly.

I took a deep breath before responding. "She said that nothing else matters, that she could take on the world so long as she had us by her side."

Rome's expression softened into a smile, clearly pleased by her response. "Guess it's not just us it's too late for, we are all down this road together," he murmured.

I nodded in agreement. "Yeah, we are. She asked me what will happen when Dominick is caught again."

Rome's arms were crossed tightly over his chest, as though he were trying to protect himself from the weight of our conversation. "How did you respond to that?" he asked, his voice cautious.

I shrugged, setting my empty cup in the sink to rinse it out. "I asked her what she wanted to happen," I said, watching the trees outside sway in the breeze. It was peaceful here, and it was easy to forget the dangers that lurked just beyond the property line.

Rome's arms remained crossed as he listened intently to my response, his eyes studying my face for any hints or clues to what Lexi had said. "I feel like you're dragging this out on purpose here," he grumbled, clearly growing impatient with my slow delivery.

I couldn't help but chuckle at his frustration, but I understood his eagerness to know more. "She doesn't want what we have started here to end once he's caught," I said, pausing to let the weight of my words sink in. "I told her we didn't either. Was I speaking for everyone?"

He didn't hesitate to confirm my statement, his voice firm and unwavering. "Of course."

As I turned to face him, I could see a flicker of uncertainty in his eyes, and I knew exactly what was on his mind. "I know you're still hesitant," I said gently. "You haven't taken it further with her."

His chuckle was laced with a hint of embarrassment, but I could tell he was trying to hide it. "I'm not as hesitant as you think," he said, his tone more serious now. "She responded so perfectly to me the other day. We just haven't had our moment yet, but I'm sure it will come soon."

I nodded in acknowledgement, a sense of relief washing over me at his words. It was comforting to know that Rome was just as invested in this as the rest of us.

Shifting the conversation away from our personal lives, I brought up the topic that always seems to dampen our moods. "Anything new on Dominick?" I asked hesitantly, knowing the answer would likely be disappointing.

Rome's expression immediately soured, his frustration palpable. "Nothing," he responded curtly. "A person like him can't just disappear off the face of the earth without some serious help. He must have someone on his payroll helping to keep him hidden. Whoever it is, they managed to keep him out of sight for more than a year last time, remember?"

I nodded slowly, feeling the weight of the situation settling heavily on my shoulders. "So he had someone as skilled as you working for him. We just have to find someone even better." I paused, gathering my thoughts. "Did you reach out to our friends?" I asked, hoping for a glimmer of hope.

Rome's lips turned up in a small, wry smile. "Yeah, I did. They can't come right away, but they'll meet up with us in four days once they're back from wherever the fuck they are right now."

I let out a small sigh of relief, grateful that we had some reinforcements on the way. "Perfect. Maybe that means we can finally end this hiding and take Lexi out into the real world," I said.

Chapter 26

Alexis

Once again, I found myself preoccupied with the men of the house. It therefore caused me to lose track of days and forget about Sam's scheduled visit. I had been sleeping in later than everyone else, but it wasn't entirely my fault, I didn't have the rigorous military training that they had, which required them to wake up early every day.

As I was about to brew some coffee, Sam suddenly appeared in the kitchen, her visit catching me off guard. She had already completed her daily routine of cleaning and laundry, and was now in the mood for some gossip before she had to leave again.

With a mischievous grin on her face, she asked me about my "super secret relationship status," teasing me in a playful manner. Despite her friendly tone, I knew that I couldn't divulge anything about the truth of my situation. To Sam, I was just an assistant helping out a group of businessmen, with a possible romantic interest in one of them, the always cheerful Hunt.

In reality, however, the men were hiding me from a dangerous and vengeful man who was intent on killing me. To complicate matters, my relationship with all of the men in the safe house was rapidly evolving into something much more than anticipated. But for the time being, I was forced to keep up the pretense and laughed along with Sam's teasing.

We sat at the dining table once again with our coffee and a slice of caramel cake while I diverted attention away from me as much as possible and Sam told me all about how Nathan decided to create some beautiful wall art for her, on her living room wall. That took her an hour to clean off.

Once she had given me a hug and wandered back out of the house to go pick up her son, I went back to what had now become my routine.

After I finished my post workout shower, I headed towards the kitchen with one thing in mind, caramel cake. But before I could get my hands on the sweet treat, I bumped into Rome as he walked out of the kitchen. Heat rushed to my cheeks as I remember the last time we were alone in the dining area.

"Hey," I said softly to him. His small smirk indicated that he might be thinking of that moment as well.

"Hey, baby girl," he replied, his voice deep and husky.

I could feel my heart flutter at the sound of his voice. "So, do I call you 'Sir' all the time now?" I asked playfully, trying to keep the atmosphere light.

He chuckled and stepped closer to me, pinning me against the wall beside the kitchen entryway. He brushed his fingers over my cheekbone, his gaze intense. "Only when we play," he whispered, his breath hot on my face.

I bit my lip, feeling a mix of excitement and apprehension. "And when will that be?" I asked, trying to act nonchalant.

Rome hummed, a small smile playing on his lips. "Whenever you want to, baby girl," he responded, his tone dripping with promise.

My heart pounded in my chest as I gathered the courage to ask the question that's been on my mind for days. "What if I want to right now?" I breathed.

Rome's smile widened, his eyes taking in every inch of me. "I would ask first if you're absolutely sure," he said, his voice low and seductive.

"Oh, absolutely sure," I replied, my voice barely above a whisper. I moved my face closer to his until our lips were almost touching. "Sir," I breathed out.

As if he had been waiting for my signal, Rome grabbed my hand firmly and pulled me towards the stairs, leading me up to the bedrooms.

As we climbed, I became aware of a noise behind me and glanced back over my shoulder. It was Gabe, who had entered the dining area from the hallway. His mouth was open, as though he was about to say something, but he quickly took in the sight of Rome's hand holding mine. His eyebrows shot up, his lips sucked between his teeth, and his eyes widened almost comically. Gabe turned around and practically scampered back down the hall, leaving us alone.

Once we reached the top of the stairs, Rome swiftly pulled me into a room that was definitely not mine. He closed the door behind us and locked it with a decisive click. His gaze intensified as he looked at me, and he raised my hand to his lips. A shiver ran down my spine as he placed a gentle kiss on the inside of my wrist.

Rome's voice was low and commanding as he spoke. "I don't have any of my normal supplies here, baby girl, so we're just going to have to make do with what we have." I have no idea what he meant, but I don't care. "Yes, Sir," I replied.

Rome released my hand and stepped away from me, his eyes roaming over my body. "Take your clothes off and lie down in the center of the bed and wait for me," he commanded.

Without hesitation, I started to undress, folding each item of clothing neatly and placing them on the armchair in the corner of the room. I knew that Rome liked to control everything around him and leaving my clothes scattered on his pristine floor would not end well for me.

At least not until I knew what kind of punishment he might dish out. Better safe than not being able to sit down for a week.

While I carefully folded each item of clothing, Rome disappeared into his closet. I couldn't see what he was doing, but he still hadn't returned by the time I had finished undressing. Following his instructions, I crawled onto the mattress and laid down on my back in the center with my head on one of the pillows. And there I waited.

And waited.

I knew Rome was testing me, but I refused to show any sign of weakness. I didn't know how long I had been lying there, but it felt like an eternity before he finally returned to the bedroom. When he walked back into the room leaving the closet light on behind him, he was carrying several items in his hands, but I couldn't see what they were.

He could have been carrying a torture device, and I still wouldn't have noticed. Because he was gloriously fucking naked. Lots of beautiful tan skin stretched over lean, powerful muscles, and my eyes hungrily traced the contours of his body.

But what had my attention, you guessed it, his beautiful fucking cock.

His beautiful Pierced. Fucking. Cock.

And no, of course he didn't just have a simple little piercing. He had a full row of barbell piercings up the underside of his cock.

A Jacob's fucking ladder.

I was dead.

I could already tell just by looking at him as he approached the bed that he was larger than any of the other men. But throw in a Jacob's fucking ladder?

Yep, I wasn't going to survive this experience. But at least I would die happy.

Despite my desire to reach out and touch him, I stayed perfectly still, waiting for him to make his next move.

He spoke up, "Do you have a safe word, baby girl?"

A safe word? Oh, that's right because he was going to kill me with his giant pierced cock but apparently I need a way to tap out.

"No," I replied, shaking my head.

Rome hummed in response as he put down whatever he was carrying on the bedside table. "Can you think of a word for me? Something you will remember but isn't something you might say normally. Something that when you say it, everything stops, because it will the moment you say it."

It was hard to concentrate on anything else with him standing there naked and within touching distance.

"Pineapple," I blurted out, without much thought.

He chuckled. "Good choice, though I distinctly recall you not really responding to Hunt's question on having a food fetish."

I furrowed my brows, trying to remember when Hunt asked me about my food fetish. Suddenly, the memory of our conversation came flooding back, it was right before he fucked me on the lounge. Rome's chuckles deepened as he saw the realization dawn on me. "There is nothing that happens in this house or outside of it that I don't see. You may not see me, but I always see you."

The thought of Rome watching me with the others through cameras I've never even noticed sent heat rushing through me. I longed to touch him, but I knew he wouldn't allow it.

"I wasn't able to watch when Gabe fucked you in the shower," Rome continued, interrupting my thoughts. "But I could still hear you. That was a new kind of torture I hadn't experienced before."

I frowned, knowing that I was not the first woman they had shared between them. "But what about-"

He cut me off by brushing his finger down the side of my face and along my jawline, then back up again. "I have never before wanted to watch every moment all of us share with a woman like I do with you."

My heart skipped a beat at his words.

Chapter 27

Alexis

"Let's go back to discussing your safeword, baby girl. Pineapple will be your safeword, but I also like to use the traffic light system. Have you heard of it?" I shook my head in response.

"If I ask you what color you are at, you are to respond with one of three options. Green means you are okay and happy to continue whatever we are doing. Yellow means you need a break or to slow down. Red means we stop and move on to aftercare. And, you don't need to wait for me to ask. If you suddenly feel the need to slow down or stop, you can simply say the color." He paused, allowing me to take it all in. "Do you understand?"

"Yes, Sir," I replied.

He hummed before asking, "What color are you at right now?"

I gave him a slow, cheeky smile and asked, "What if I want to say pink?"

His lip twitched, and he raised an eyebrow at me before replying, "Then that is the color I will turn your ass into for being a brat."

His response caused my breath to stutter, and I could feel myself almost dripping for him at his words.

"What color are you at? And do not make me ask again," he commanded.

"Green, Sir," I replied.

"Good girl," he praised.

It's official; I definitely had a praise kink. Those two simple words said by him in that husky voice almost made me cum.

"Hands out in front of you." he commanded.

I complied and raised them in the air. He took my hands in his, the sensation of his warm touch sending shivers down my spine. He folded one hand over the other before proceeding to wrap a length of material around my wrists. The material was tight enough to ensure I couldn't escape, but not so tight that it was painful. It felt restrictive, yet exhilarating at the same time.

My heart raced as he took the end of another piece of fabric and threaded it through the material around my wrist, almost like a lead. I felt a gentle tug as he tightened it, but it was still not so tight that I felt like objecting. The sensation of being bound was both exhilarating and nerve-wracking.

With the other end of the fabric, he pulled my arms above my head and tied them tightly to one of the bars that ran along the head of the bed. I couldn't move my arms, and it sent a shiver down my spine. He tested the security of the knot with an experimental tug and then checked to ensure that it was not too tight around my wrists.

I couldn't help but wonder if this was a regular setup on his bed, and if he did this with other women. The thought of him using this setup with someone else sparked a sudden surge of possessive jealousy that I wasn't prepared for.

He paused to examine my face, perhaps detecting something in my expression. "Color?" he asked.

I whispered, "Green, sir."

He tilted his head, appearing somewhat skeptical. "What's the matter?"

I struggled to admit my growing possessiveness towards them, my jealousy threatened to transform me into a green-eyed monster at the mere idea of them being intimate with someone else. "I was just wondering if your bed is always arranged like this when you're with others."

His face momentarily betrayed a fleeting emotion before he seized my chin, exerting pressure with his fingers.

"No," he snapped at me. "We won't do that anymore. From this moment on, there was no one before you, and there will be no one after you. Do you understand?"

I reluctantly nodded my head.

"And, baby girl, if I hear you speak like that again or insinuate any uncertainty about what we have established here, I'll turn your butt so red that you won't be able to sit for a week."

Holy. Fuck.

My entire body felt like it was on fire, and the dampness between my legs became even more intense. The ache in my pussy was almost unbearable, and I couldn't resist the urge to rub my thighs together to create some much-needed friction. But before I could even begin to find relief, I felt a sharp slap on my leg, causing me to gasp in surprise.

"What is the rule, baby girl?" he growled, his fingers gently caressing the stinging area.

I whimpered in response, my voice barely above a whisper. "No cumming without permission."

He hummed thoughtfully, his hand moving up my thigh and towards the apex of my legs. "Do I need to restrain your legs too or will you behave for me?"

The idea of being restrained sent shivers down my spine, but I knew that I wanted to please him. "I'll be a good girl, Sir," I replied, my voice breathy and full of desire. I was so turned on that I wouldn't be surprised if I was already making a mess on his bed.

He moved around the bed slowly, his eyes fixed on me with an intensity that I felt all over my body. As he reached the end of the bed, he leaned down and wrapped his strong hands around my ankles, his grip was firm and possessive. He pulled me towards him, tugging my body closer to the center of the bed. I felt the restraints on my wrists tighten, and I knew that I was completely at his mercy now.

The sensation of being restrained was both thrilling and terrifying, and I couldn't help but feel a rush of excitement as he looked me up and down, his eyes filled with lust and desire. I was vulnerable, exposed, and completely at his mercy.

"You look so beautiful like this," he murmured, his voice low and seductive. "All tied up and at my mercy."

I gasped at his words, feeling a surge of desire wash over me. This was what I'd been craving, the feeling of complete surrender to his will. I wanted him to take control of my body, to use me for his pleasure.

He leant forward, his hand trailing up my leg in a slow, teasing motion. "But don't worry, baby girl," he added, his tone playful now. "I promise to be gentle. For now."

I moaned softly at his touch, my body arching towards him as he explored every inch of my exposed skin. I was completely under his spell, lost in the sensation of his touch and the heady rush of submission.

And then, with a sudden tug on my ankles, he pulled my legs apart, leaving me completely exposed to his gaze. I felt a surge of self-consciousness wash over me, but I knew that I couldn't resist him. I was his to command, his to use, his to pleasure. And I wouldn't have it any other way.

Instead of directing his attention to my pussy, he turned his focus to my ankle. As he lifted it up, his face descended to it, pressing a soft kiss to the skin. He released my other ankle and began to lightly brush his fingers up the inside of the leg he was concentrating on. As his fingers swept over the extra sensitive flesh at my knee, my leg twitched involuntarily, but he continued on, making it to the skin on the inside of my thigh before returning down my leg. This time, he paused at my knee as the hand around my ankle moved up towards it, pushing my leg out further.

He leant forward and gently kissed the side of my knee, teasingly close to the most sensitive spot, causing me to almost sigh. Then he licked a solid line along the sensitive flesh, eliciting a moan as my pussy throbbed and clenched in response. His eyes briefly flicked to mine before returning to his task as he lowered my leg back down to the bed. He then moved to repeat the same process with my other leg.

I felt the same sweet kisses against my skin, the smooth glide of his hands as he opened my legs further, and the long lick to my sensitive skin. This time, my back arched as I shifted slightly, seeking any relief without being punished for it. He hummed and his lips tugged up at the corner, catching me trying to get away with something.

As he knelt between my legs on the bed, his hands slid up the inside of my thighs. His thumbs swept softly on the skin at the crease of my thighs, tracing the path he licked the last time he was between them. The sensation sent shivers down my spine, and I could feel myself getting wetter. He swept his fingers up my pussy, gathering my wetness and then brought his finger up to suck into his mouth. He groaned as his eyes fluttered closed briefly, then lazily blinked open, his fingers went back down to slide through my wetness again.

"I was already missing the taste of you, baby girl. Have you ever tasted yourself before?" he asked, and I shook my head slightly. He rested a hand on the bed beside my body before leaning forward, sliding his wet fingers into my panting mouth.

"Suck," he commanded, and I did as he said. The flavor of myself burst across my tongue, surprisingly sweet and not at all what I was expecting. He dragged his fingers back out of my mouth and rested his hand on the mattress beside my head. He lowered his body until it brushed only softly against mine, until his face was hovering close enough for our noses to brush against one another.

He was so tall that in this position, the tip of his cock rested perfectly against my clit. Even the simple twitch of it made my pussy throb with desire. He teased his tongue against my bottom lip before sliding it inside my mouth, chasing the taste of me he just gave me. It was the first full kiss he had given me, and he didn't disappoint. His tongue and lips consumed me, devouring my mouth and swallowing the whimper that left me at the possession his kiss offered.

He slowly retreated after the kiss, giving me a couple of soft brushing kisses. He then raised himself up and slid back down the bed, kneeling between my legs once again. Moving onto his elbows, he brought his face closer to me and slid his hands under my ass, lifting my pussy directly to his face.

With the same thoroughness as he did with my mouth, he devoured my pussy. His tongue moved through my folds, circling and flicking my clit before plunging inside me as he sucked and consumed my wetness. His lips closed over my clit and sucked it while his tongue flicked at it.

He released it again and slid his mouth back down, gathering the new wetness on his tongue as he went back to licking my pussy.

"Cum for me baby girl, you need to cum one time before I can give you my cock," he murmured before closing his lips around my clit again, sucking hard.

My orgasm exploded out of me and my back arched as I moaned loudly. My wrists tugged against their restraints as they stopped me from reaching down as my body pulsed around nothing but air.

Chapter 28

Alexis

As he settled back onto his knees, he glided his fingers through my slick folds, relishing in the way I shivered at his touch. He then wrapped his hand around his own hardness, tracing his fingers up and down his length with a tantalizing slowness that left me breathless. "Do you want this, baby girl? Do you want me to be buried deep inside you?" he murmured, his voice thick with desire.

I nodded eagerly, my breath hitching in my throat as I watched him stroke his cock with one hand. Suddenly, a sharp slap to my thigh broke my trance, causing me to gasp. "Yes, Sir," I stammered, my heart pounding with anticipation.

"Beg for it," he commanded, his eyes locked onto mine.

"Please, Sir," I whispered, my voice barely audible. "I need you inside me."

He hummed, his hand still moving along his length. "I'm not sure that was good enough. Maybe you don't want this after all," he said, teasingly.

Desperate to have him inside me, I pleaded with him. "Please, Sir. Please give me your cock," I whimpered, my voice trembling with need.

Satisfied with my response, he shuffled forward until he was using his knees to hold my legs open, the tip of him brushing against me. He pressed a hand to the mattress beside my waist, steadying himself as he used his other hand to guide the head of his cock through my wet folds.

Locking eyes with me, he demanded, "Color, baby girl."

"Green," I replied breathlessly, feeling my body thrum with excitement. "God, so fucking green, Sir."

He wordlessly began to push inside of me, starting slowly and deliberately, each inch of him causing a delightful burn that stretched me in the most pleasurable way. As he thrust deeper, I felt his piercings rub against my sensitive walls, sending electrifying shivers down my spine. Eventually, he buried himself completely inside me and leaned over to plant his other hand on the mattress on my other side.

"Wrap your legs around me," he ordered, his eyes burning with desire.

Obeying him without hesitation, I spread my hips as far as I could and coiled my legs around his waist. He adjusted his position and then started dragging his cock out of me until only the tip remained.

Oh. My. Fucking. God.

The burning sensation was gone now, and all I could feel was him. His piercings made each movement feel exquisitely intense. A loud moan escaped my lips, but I was not alone.

"God, you feel fucking incredible," he breathed.

With a slow and deliberate pace, he pushed himself back inside of me, withdrawing just as slowly before repeating the motion. Each time he did, my body responded with gasps and moans, as the sensations he elicited were beyond anything I could have imagined. I could feel another orgasm starting to build inside of me, and as he continued to move in and out of my body with excruciating slowness, my pussy tightened around him, aching for release.

"Please, Sir," I begged, unable to hold back any longer.

"Don't you dare fucking cum," he ordered, his voice filled with authority.

I whimpered in response, my body tightened even further around his cock. The orgasm that had been building inside of me became almost impossible to hold off any longer, and I knew that I was on the brink of climax. But just as I was about to let go, he pulled out of me completely, and I whined in disappointment at the loss of both him and the orgasm that had slipped away.

Without warning, he pulled my legs from around himself and swung one of them over to the other side. Using the momentum of my body, he grabbed my hips and rolled me onto my stomach. It became clear to me that he had tied my wrists in a specific way, as the roll of my body had no effect on how they were secured or how they felt around my wrists.

He straddled my legs and cupped the curves of my ass with his hands, sliding them further up before giving both cheeks a firm squeeze, one after the other. Suddenly, he landed a slap against my right cheek, and the sting and burn of it reignited the retreating orgasm. He repeated the action on my other cheek, causing me to moan softly, while his hands rubbed the burn.

"Fuck, your ass looks so pretty in pink, baby girl," he murmured, admiring his handiwork.

He positioned himself between my legs once more, and with one hand, he moved them apart, while lifting my hips slightly. Suddenly, he plunged back inside of me. This angle was even tighter than before, and the sensation of his piercings against the front wall of my pussy was beyond words. I was left breathless, unable to catch my breath. He definitely picked the wrong position if he was hoping to slow down my orgasm.

"Oh my god!" I cried out.

He continued his agonizingly slow movements, entering and retreating from my pussy, and my orgasm raged back to life. I couldn't hold back any longer.

"Please Sir, can I cum? Please?" I begged.

He lowered his body against mine, resting his elbows on either side of my chest. Using one knee, he bent my leg out to the side, allowing him to push deeper inside me at a slightly different angle.

"Cum for me, baby girl," he ordered.

I couldn't resist any longer. I was clenching and pulsing around him before he even finished speaking. The scream that escaped me was so loud it echoed around the room as my orgasm tore through me.

As my pussy slowly relaxed around him, he shifted his body closer to mine and rolled his hips in a short, shallow thrust. The sensation sent shivers down my spine and caused me to moan uncontrollably. He repeated the motion, rolling his hips back and then thrusting forward once more, establishing a slow yet powerful rhythm. With every thrust, I felt his balls slap against my pussy, sending waves of pleasure throughout my body.

He reached out and grabbed a handful of my hair, pulling my head back to meet his. I felt his tongue flick at the corner of my mouth as I panted and moaned. "Does that feel good, baby girl? Do you like my cock in your tight little pussy?" he asked.

I whispered in response, my body tightened around him yet again. "Yes, Sir," I managed to say.

He asked me, "What's your color?"

"Green, Sir," I answered breathlessly.

"Do you want to cum again? Should I let you cum again?" he asked.

"Yes, please Sir, please," I pleaded.

Suddenly, he stopped, and my orgasm faded away.

"No!" I whimpered in protest, and he responded by giving me a sharp slap on my leg. Then, while still buried deep inside me, he rolled us over, causing my back to arch completely. Our cheeks rubbed against each other, and I was lost in pleasure once more.

He slid his arm around and up the center of my body, wrapping his hand around my throat firmly, making it harder for me to breathe. His other hand traveled down my front, feeling the curves of my body until it reached the spot where his cock was buried deep inside me. He pulled out slowly before slamming back into me with force, making me scream.

He rolled his hips back, slowly withdrawing before thrusting up into me again. The sensation was overwhelming as his piercings scraped against the front of my pussy while the head of his cock rubbed directly against my G-spot. I couldn't help but cry out in pleasure as he repeated the motion, each thrust sending shockwaves through my body. I could barely catch my breath before he tightened his grip around my throat and lifted me up, arching my back even further. His other hand left my body and started circling my clit, sending waves of pleasure throughout me.

The intensity of the stimulation was too much for me to bear, and tears streamed down my face. He didn't stop, though, and started thrusting harder and faster, making my body bounce with every impact.

"Do you want me to come deep inside this pussy, baby girl? Want me to fill up this pretty little pussy with my cum?" His deep husky voice had me clenching around him.

"Yes! Please Sir, yes." I begged, my voice was a desperate whine.

With his own breathing becoming ragged and his hard pace losing its rhythm, his voice took on a harsh growl. "You want my cum so deep inside you that you'll be dripping with it for days?" he asked.

My body hovered on the edge, aching for release. "Please, please, please!" I cried out in desperation.

"Cum now," He demanded.

With a sudden and powerful intensity, my orgasm hit me like a sledgehammer, reverberating through my entire body and causing me to shatter around him. The pleasure was so intense that I couldn't help but let out a loud and unbridled scream. As I writhed and trembled in ecstasy, I could sense that he'd reached the peak of his own pleasure as well. With a rough groan, he exploded deep inside me, his release adding to the already overwhelming sensation.

Despite my awareness of his own climax, I was completely consumed by the tornado of pleasure that had overtaken me. It was like a wild and chaotic wind that swept me up like a helpless ragdoll, throwing me into the air and tossing me around. I was lost in a world of pure sensation, with no thought or awareness of anything else beyond the overwhelming pleasure that engulfed me.

I came down from the earth shattering moment to Rome rolling me onto my side and slowly untying my hands, rubbing along my skin where the material was wrapped tightly around them.

He leaned in, gently brushing the stray strands of hair away from my face, before pulling me up into a sitting position. His warm touch sent a shiver down my spine as he held an open water bottle to my lips, allowing me to take small sips of the refreshing liquid. Once I'd quenched my thirst, he gently lowered me back onto the soft mattress.

As he disappeared into the bathroom, I took a moment to catch my breath and center myself. When he returned, he carried a warm wet cloth that he used to clean my sensitive areas, the tender skin causing me to whimper as he gently cleaned me. "I know baby girl, just a couple more moments," he reassured me, his voice was a soothing balm to my raw nerves.

He continued to wipe me down with the cloth, his gentle touch moved from my thighs up to my chest and down to my toes. Each time he changed the cloth, he made me stop to take another sip from the water bottle, his praise a constant

stream of encouragement. "You're such a good girl," he murmured, his words a soft caress against my skin.

Finally, he finished and returned to the bed, cradling me in
his strong arms. His soft praise continued as he ran his hands
over my spine, coaxing my body to relax and let go, drifting
off into a peaceful sleep.

Chapter 29

Rome

A piercing, deafening noise and bright lights jolted me awake from a deep sleep. A really loud fucking noise.

The sound of an alarm screeched throughout the entire house startled me more than my security system turning all the lights on, and before my mind could even fully come online, I was already up and out of bed, adrenaline pumping through my veins. I forcefully yanked open the drawer next to me, hastily pulling on the bulletproof vest and pants I kept there, then reached for the loaded gun.

As I quickly scanned the room, I noticed that Lexi was mirroring my every move on the other side of the bed. The gorgeous and intelligent woman knew we had emergency supplies on both sides of the bed, in case something like this were to happen. For us, the saying "getting out of the wrong side of the bed" simply did not apply. Even though the clothes were too large for her, they would have to suffice.

Just as I reached the laptop I'd placed on the side of the room, my door slammed open and Colt charged in, making a beeline for Lexi. He shot me a perplexed look, as if asking what we were up against. I was just as clueless as he was.

After a quick assessment, I realized that the alarm was triggered by something, yet when I checked all the cameras, there was no sign of any disturbance. Everything appeared to be in order and mundane.

I pressed the button on the monitor, cycling through a different set of cameras, hoping to find some clue as to what triggered the alarm. However, as the footage played out before me, my confusion deepened. There was nothing unusual to be seen. No movement, no disturbances, and certainly no intruders.

Hunt and Gabe had joined us in the room now, with Hunt quickly moving towards Lexi, who was as composed as ever. Meanwhile, Gabe stood beside me, studying the camera feed with hawk-like intensity. Even though I was confident that I hadn't missed anything, Gabe's thoroughness was reassuring.

I started to cycle through the cameras again, hoping that a slower approach might yield some answers. I studied each angle in detail, looking for any anomalies or changes that may have gone unnoticed before. Despite my meticulous search, I was left empty-handed.

As I continued to study the camera feeds, frustration and unease continued to bubble inside me. This was not how my security system was supposed to function. My mind raced, trying to identify any possible gaps or weaknesses in my security measures. I was determined to get to the bottom of this, to figure out what triggered the alarm and why.

Suddenly, Colt's voice cut through my thoughts. "Go back," he said, pointing at something on the screen. I complied, rewinding the footage until we reached the moment just before the alarm was triggered. And there, amidst the usual static images of empty hallways and locked doors, something caught my eye.

I focused intently on the blurry image that Colt had pointed out, squinting as I tried to make out the details on the screen. Initially, I had dismissed it as an animal due to its size and heat signature but upon closer inspection, I realized my mistake. It seemed like a jumbled mess of metal and plastic against one of the perimeter gates.

"Shit."

I quickly switched to the long-range cameras, scanning through them at lightning speed until I spotted a car speeding away from the scene. Without wasting any time, I took a screenshot before it disappeared from the camera's range.

I turned to Colt, who was already focused on me, then shifted my gaze to Lexi. Despite the alarming situation, she remained unfazed and resolute, displaying a determined expression on her face.

It was ironic that our entire reason for being here was to ensure her safety and protect her, yet she exhibited a strength and steeliness that was impressive.

Sensing my unspoken message, Colt turned to Lexi, his hand cupping her neck as he drew her closer to him.

"Don't worry, princess. Whatever it was, it's gone now. Why don't you let the twins take you back to your room and get some rest?" He gave her a brief kiss before passing her over to Gabe's waiting arms.

Hunt and Gabe took the hint and started ushering her from the room but she stopped them briefly just inside the door to look at us. "Are we safe here, can they get in?"

She wasn't just concerned about herself here, she wanted to know that we were all safe. My heart squeezed in my chest.

"We're safe, baby girl, get some rest and we will talk about it again later today after you've had some more sleep."

My assurance seemed to placate her and she let the twins pull her from the room.

We waited until we heard her door close and I brought up the camera in her room in the corner of my screen to see Gabe and Hunt helping her out of the ill fitting vest and pants and into some more comfortable clothes that fit.

Colt broke the silence, his voice low and serious. "Are we safe?"

I paused before answering, taking a moment to gather my thoughts. "For now, yes. They couldn't penetrate the security system, but they definitely tried," I replied.

"Dominick?" he questioned, and I nodded in agreement.

"My guess is he hired some professionals," I replied.

"Question is, how did they find us?" he mused, his eyes scanning the screens for any clues.

I furrowed my brow, deep in thought. "There was nothing left on camera about her and connecting her to us."

"Something doesn't feel right," Colt murmured, and I could feel the tension in the air thickening.

"Agreed," I said, nodding in understanding.

"I'm guessing you're not going back to sleep?" Colt asked, knowing that I wouldn't be able to rest until we had more answers.

I shook my head, already beginning to pull up the necessary information on my computer. "I'll start digging into this and then check out the remains at the gate at first light," I informed him, pointing to the image still displayed on my screen.

"Don't bring it inside the perimeter, we can't chance that it's a Trojan horse. Just document and destroy," Colt warned.

I nodded in agreement and gave him a two-finger salute, already immersed in the task. I heard the soft sound of him leaving the room as I focused on gathering any piece of information that could help us identify our intruders.

Moments later, I saw him walking into Lexi's room, taking up his usual spot in the armchair in the corner of the room. I knew he wouldn't be sleeping either; he was there to watch over her like some mythical superhero.

I kept searching and working but found no leads and the hours passed by quickly until the first rays of sunlight finally started to brighten the sky.

I quickly pulled a shirt over the vest I had been wearing and grabbed some of my equipment before exiting my room. Gabe was waiting for me at the top of the stairs, and we exchanged a silent nod before making our way out of the house. The tension was palpable, and I could tell that none of us got any more sleep after the incident last night. It was too close, too sudden, and too unsettling for any of us to feel at ease.

We didn't have to search for long before we came across the mangled wreckage near one of the gates. It was immediately clear that it had once been a remote control car or something similar. Gabe looked at me expectantly, waiting for me to give some insight.

"It's some sort of remote control device," I said, examining the wreckage with my equipment. But there was nothing that my scanners could pick up. It was almost as if someone had aimed a kid's toy at the wall and left it there after it blew up on contact with the security system. In the middle of the night.

After finishing my inspection, I turned to Gabe and said, "There's nothing to get from it. It's all yours."

With a mischievous grin, Gabe took the device from me and led us a short distance away from the gate, ensuring we were still concealed from public view. I watched him, but I didn't need to see what he was doing to know what was about to happen.

Moments later, he turned back to me and signaled for us to move further away. We had barely reached the gate again when I heard a loud crack followed by a sharp boom behind us, a wave of hot air hitting us for a moment before vanishing.

"Fuck, Gabe, what was that?" I asked, startled.

He cackled. "Just something a friend gave me."

I groaned, feeling a mixture of annoyance and amusement. "We need to stop you two from spending time together. Is that going to set fire to the trees?"

Gabe continued to chuckle. "Nah, it was contained."

I shook my head, both exasperated and amused, as we both moved through the gate and I secured it behind us again.

As we made our way back into the house, the sun had fully risen, casting a bright light over everything in its path. Gabe wasted no time and rushed upstairs to check on Lexi, while I headed towards the kitchen to get my much-needed coffee fix. In the kitchen, Colt was already there, gazing out the window at the trees outside, lost in thought.

"Did you find anything?" he asked me without diverting his gaze from the window.

"Unfortunately, nothing," I replied, with a hint of disappointment audible in my voice.

Colt nodded, comprehending my frustration. "Is our security still intact?" he questioned.

"Yes, we're still secure, but I'll be more attentive. We need to remain vigilant until our friends arrive," I affirmed.

He acknowledged my statement with a nod.

"Speaking of our friends, it seems like Gabe had acquired some new toys that go boom," I informed him.

Colt let out a bark of laughter and shook his head in amusement. "Of course he had. Why am I not surprised?" he remarked, still chuckling.

I grinned at him mischievously. "Maybe we shouldn't leave those two unsupervised moving forward," I suggested, half-jokingly.

"Good luck with that," Colt responded, his lips curving into a smirk. "I'd love to see you try and tell them what to do."

I chuckled at that.

Once Colt finished his coffee he washed out his mug and placed it carefully on the drying rack before he took a deep breath and looked at me with determination in his eyes, "Now wish me luck. I need to shuffle our workload around, as I don't think we'll be able to finish our upcoming jobs with the current situation."

My face contorted into a grimace as I responded, "Well, good luck with that."

Chapter 30

Alexis

In the afternoon, I was en route to the gym for my regular workout when I heard an exasperated growl emanating from the open door of the office. As a result, my feet instinctively took me towards the source of the noise. Peering into the doorway, I spotted Colt sitting behind the desk, completely engrossed in the laptop in front of him. He was rubbing his forehead with one hand, as if experiencing physical discomfort.

As soon as I stepped inside and closed the door, Colt's attention was drawn towards me. "Hey, princess," he greeted me with a sigh.

"Hey, are you okay?" I asked with concern etched on my face.

He gave me a reassuring smile. "Nothing I can't handle."

I walked over to the desk and leaned against it while he turned his chair towards me. "You know you can talk to me, right? A different perspective might be helpful."

He chuckled, his eyes scanning my workout outfit before meeting my gaze again. "I know that, princess. If it was something you could help me with, I would definitely ask. I'm just trying to finish shifting some jobs around while I wait for a call."

His response made me frown, and I tilted my head as I pondered what he had just said. "Is this because of me? Shouldn't you be working on other jobs right now? Am I causing a problem for you?"

He grasped my chin as I looked down, directing me to look at him directly. "No, don't do that. I've said it before, and I'll say it a million times, your safety is our top priority. I couldn't care less about those other jobs; there are other teams who can handle them. You come first."

Our gazes remained locked in an intense stare, and my heart pounded faster in my chest as I leaned forward to press my lips against his in a delicate and affectionate kiss. He responded with the same tenderness, his fingers gently traced the curve of my neck and sent electric jolts of pleasure down my spine.

When we broke apart, I stood up straight and leaned over him, resting my hands on the armrests of his chair.

I spoke up, my voice soft and sincere. "Have I thanked you for everything you're doing for me?"

A small smile tugged at the corners of his lips. "No, I don't think you have."

I chuckled, brushing my lips against his again before pulling back slightly. He tried to follow, but I pressed my hands against his chest, keeping him in his seat. "Well then, thank you. I really appreciate everything you're doing for me."

As his smile grew wider, the stress that had etched lines into his face just moments ago seemed to fade away

I leaned in again, planting soft kisses along his jawline and down his neck. His breath caught in his throat as I moved lower, brushing my lips across his collarbone and down his chest. I could feel the tension in his body as I knelt before him, my hands trailed down his chest and abdomen until I reached the waistband of his pants. He then choked on his own breath as with a deft movement, I undid his zipper and pulled his cock free from his boxers. It was already hard and throbbing.

"What are you doing, princess?" His voice was husky, and the roughness of his tone sent shivers down my spine. But this wasn't about me.

"Showing my appreciation," I murmured in reply. With a mischievous glint in my eye, I leaned in closer to him, taking in the heady scent of his arousal. My tongue snaked out, tracing a line all the way from the base of his shaft to the tip, eliciting a deep groan from deep within his chest. I continued to tease him with the tip of my tongue, flicking it across the head of his cock, feeling it grow harder in response. His hands gripped the arms of his chair tightly, knuckles turning white with the force of his hold.

With another low groan, his head fell back against the top of the office chair, his body sinking deeper into it. "Holy fuck," he breathed out in a husky tone. I slid his pants down just enough to give me unrestricted access to him, and then ran my tongue over him once more, savoring the taste of his skin. As I took him deep into my mouth, his tip brushed against the back of my throat, making me moan softly in response. Wrapping my hand around his base, I squeezed gently, reveling in the feel of him.

"Fuck, your mouth feels so fucking good," he groaned, his words laced with pleasure.

I hollowed my cheeks and started to move up and down his length, my tongue playing along the underside of him as I went. He groaned in pleasure, his grip on the chair tightened so hard that I heard something crack, but I didn't stop. Instead, I moved my mouth up and down his length, my tongue traced every inch of him. I could feel him twitch and grow even harder in response.

As I reached over to move his hands to the top of my head, he pulled my hair tie out and wound his fingers into my long locks, taking a firm hold. He began to flex his hips, guiding me to take him deeper and deeper with each thrust.

"Open your gorgeous throat and breathe through your nose, princess," he commanded, his voice thick with desire. "I want to feel you swallow around my fucking cock."

I complied and felt him pushing further and deeper with each thrust until his cock was buried so far down my throat that my nose brushed against his pelvis. Every few thrusts, he held his cock deep inside me, and I swallowed around him before he pulled back to let me breathe. Thank god for my lack of gag reflex.

As he continued to fuck my mouth, he let out a contant stream of filth. "Fuck! This goddamn mouth! God, you were made to take my cock, weren't you, princess? You're sucking my cock so fucking good." His dirty talk was just making me wetter by the second.

Suddenly, his phone rang and he growled in frustration. "Fuck! I need to take this."

As he tried to pull my head off his cock, I resisted, feeling a sharp twinge of pain as he tugged on my hair. I glanced up at him with a mischievous grin and his eyes widened in surprise as he fumbled with his phone one-handed. With his cock still in my mouth, I slid my tongue along the underside of him and he moaned, nearly choking as the call connected on speakerphone and he cleared his throat.

"Kacey," he managed to say.

I nearly choked myself as my eyes widened in surprise.

"Colt, how are you doing?" came the voice from the phone.

It seemed I was in for a penny, as they say. I resumed sucking on his cock, but at a slower pace.

"I'm getting there," Colt responded to Kacey's question, but I knew his words were directed at me as he tightened his grip on my hair, causing me to moan softly around his cock. The vibrations from my moan made him thrust deeper into my throat.

Hmmm, what are the chances Kacey couldn't hear me sucking Colt's dick?

"And how is Lexi?" Kacey asked.

Did I regret ignoring Colt's attempt to stop me when he answered the call? Definitely fucking not.

But did I regret having to listen to my ex while I was deepthroating Colt? Hell fucking yes.

"She's good," Colt's response was neutral, but when I looked up at him, he mumbled under his breath so that only I can hear, "So fucking good."

"That's great, I was worried by now she would be going mad with cabin fever. She can be a bit of a brat when she wants," Kacey chuckled, oblivious to what was happening on

Colt's end of the line. I narrowed my eyes in the direction of the phone, considering interrupting the conversation to give Kacey a piece of my mind.

Colt tightened his hand and thrust into my throat again, forcing me to swallow him down. He held me there, pressing my nose into his skin as he spoke into the phone. "No, she has found things to occupy herself with."

Kacey chuckled. "Good then. So, just a quick update on where we are at."

Colt tapped something on his phone as he pulled me off his cock by my hair, growling. "It's on mute, princess," he told me as my eyes flicked to the phone on his desk. I heard Kacey continue talking. "Now you're going to let me fuck your throat until I cum, and you better swallow every drop. Before I have to take it back off mute."

He pushed me back down with a grunted "Open" and thrust his cock back into my mouth, making good on his promise. His thrusts were almost brutal as he kept my head exactly where he wanted it. Kacey's voice became nothing more than a dull murmur in the background as I moaned and whimpered with every movement of his cock.

"Such a good fucking girl, swallowing my cock," he growled, "Do you like choking on it, princess? Are you dripping for me?"

Oh, hell yes.

His pace faltered, and his thrusts lost their rhythm mere moments before his gravelly groans filled the air. "Fuck, I'm cumming. Swallow every fucking drop, princess," he commanded, his voice deep and demanding.

I eagerly complied, savoring the taste of him as his hot cum exploded down my throat, eliciting a moan of pleasure from me. I sucked at him hungrily, determined to take every last drop.

He gently pulled me back, just in time for me to hear Kacey's voice calling out to him, checking if he was still on the line. I darted forward and gave him one final lick, earning a low growl and a warning glare as he took the phone off mute and resumed his conversation.

Chapter 31

Alexis

I slowly rose to my feet, my knees feeling a bit unsteady from kneeling for so long, I caught his intense gaze fixed on me, like a predator eyeing its prey. But I flashed him a mischievous grin and quickly fixed my hair before making my way to the door, leaving him to his conversation.

However, Colt had other plans. I heard him hastily ending his call with Kacey before he swiftly followed me. Before I could even open the door more than a few inches, his hand slammed against it, forcing it shut with a loud thud.

He swiftly turned me around to face him, and I felt small under his towering presence as he leaned over me, bracing his arms against the door on either side of my head. I couldn't help but notice that he had already put himself away in the few seconds that my back was turned.

With a growl, he leaned in close to me and asked, "Did you seriously think I wouldn't be returning the favor, princess?"

Before I even had a chance to respond, he dropped to his knees and violently pulled down my leggings and underwear in one swift tug. With one leg lifted and then the other, he removed the material and tossed it over his shoulder. As he threw the leg he was holding over his shoulder, I slapped my hands against the door to steady myself, the sound reverberating through the quiet room.

His gaze hungrily fixated on my exposed pussy, and he let out a loud groan before he reached forward to slowly glide his fingers through my wetness, then plunged two fingers deep inside me.

"Look at that pretty fucking pussy. So wet for me. Is this all from sucking my cock, princess?" he asked, his hunger evident in his eyes.

I let out a moan as his mouth closed over my clit, and all rational thought disappeared. He skillfully moved his mouth over me, flicking my clit, sliding through my folds, and thrusting deep into me with his tongue while his fingers followed the same paths. My hips involuntarily rocked into his face and my hands clutched at his head, trying to pull at his short hair but without success. The sound of his fingers and mouth on me were almost obscene.

I could feel myself tightening around his fingers as he thrust them into me, his mouth latching once again onto my clit.

Colt's skilled mouth and fingers continued to work their magic on me, driving me to the edge of pleasure.

Suddenly, someone knocked on the door, interrupting us.

I cursed, loudly, "Jesus fucking Christ! Go away!"

Despite the interruption, Colt chuckled against my pussy but didn't stop, the amazing man that he was.

"Ummm." It was one of the twins, though I couldn't tell which one, and I didn't give a damn at that moment.

"If you don't leave right fucking now I will kill you and you know I know how!" I snapped.

I heard a loud laugh from the other side of the door before it went silent, and I assumed that they had left, but it's possible that they were still lurking outside, listening in. Frankly, I didn't care either way. At that moment, I was completely focused on the intense sensations coursing through my body, and I didn't care one bit about the possibility of an audience.

"Don't fucking stop or I'll stab you too," I snarled at him, half-jokingly but also deadly serious in my need for him to keep going.

He chuckled again but started moving and licking and sucking harder, and I let out a loud moan that could probably have been heard throughout the entire house. My pussy had tightened so hard around his fingers that I was surprised he could still move them.

As Colt's fingers found my G-spot and his mouth sucked hard on my clit, his teeth grazing against it, I shattered into a million pieces. My body convulsed with pleasure, tightening and releasing repeatedly around his fingers, and I could feel myself dripping down my leg.

"Fuck yes! Colt!" I cried out, my voice almost a scream.

He continued to lick my pussy a few more times before he stood up and pressed his body against mine, supporting me against the door. It was a good thing he did because my legs felt like they might give out any second.

"You are my new favorite flavor. I don't think I'll ever get enough of the taste of you, princess," he whispered in my ear.

His strong hands firmly gripped the sides of my neck, his thumbs traced a path over my cheekbones, as he passionately kissed me, devouring my mouth with the same passion he just devoured my pussy. I could taste myself on him. I could feel my heart racing and my body trembling with pleasure as his lips moved hungrily against mine.

As he pulled away, a sly smirk spread across his face, his eyes gleaming mischievously. "Your appreciation is duly noted," he said, his voice low and husky. "We will have to revisit this if I ever feel unappreciated again."

With a chuckle, he released me and sauntered back to his desk, his gaze never left mine. I let out a deep groan and slumped against the door, my body still buzzed from the intense pleasure he had just bestowed upon me.

Slowly, I gathered my wits and reached down to pick up my leggings, pulling them back up over my hips. He was still laughing softly to himself as he settled back into his office chair, and I couldn't help but feel a sense of annoyance mixed with amusement. With a sly grin, I grabbed the pair of underwear that I had left on the floor and flung them directly at his face before turning and flinging the door open, striding out of the room, relishing in the sound of his booming laughter as it rang out behind me.

My feet didn't even falter at the sight of Gabe leaning against the wall outside the office with a grin a mile wide across his face.

Without acknowledging his presence, I walked towards the dining area and slumped into a chair beside Rome, who was busy typing away on his computer.

I felt my cheeks flush with a deep shade of crimson as I tried to maintain my composure in front of him. Despite my best efforts, I could sense the heat radiating from my face as I caught him stifling a laugh. His eyes twinkled with amusement, and I couldn't help but shoot him a sarcastic glare.

After struggling to contain his amusement, he eventually managed to suppress his laughter, and an uneasy silence fell between us. However, he quickly interrupted the stillness with a playful question, "Hey, did you happen to skip your workout today?" His mischievous tone suggested that he already knew the answer. Suddenly, he burst out laughing, the sound bounced off the walls and echoed throughout the wide-open space.

Despite feeling somewhat embarrassed, I remained composed and waited patiently for him to finish laughing at my expense. It took a few moments, but when his laughter finally subsided into chuckles, I responded with a dry wit that caught him off guard. "Well, actually, I do feel like I got a nice workout while I swallowed Colt's cock," I said, giving him a sardonic look. "Sir."

He choked on his laughter, caught off guard by my blunt response. I could sense his desire building, but he quickly composed himself and shot me a heated look before settling back down to work in silence.

The silence stretched between us, each lost in our own thoughts, and time seemed to pass agonizingly slowly. Eventually, he broke the stillness once more with a soft inquiry, "How are you doing after last night, baby girl?"

His words evoked a crimson blush that spread across my cheeks, causing me to clear my throat in an attempt to regain my composure. "Umm, really good," I replied with a small smile.

A mischievous grin tugged at his lips as he clarified his question. "I meant after the alarm," he said, and my smile quickly faded as the memory of the previous night flooded back into my mind.

"Oh, yeah, I'm okay," I replied, trying to sound more confident than I felt. "I mean, I had hoped that he wouldn't find me, but I knew there was always a chance."

He paused his work to look at me intently, concern etched on his face. "I don't think it's actually Dominick himself," he said slowly. "I think he paid a lot of money for someone else to find you." I nodded, my thoughts already having led me to the same conclusion. I knew that Dominick had significant resources at his disposal, given how he had managed to track me down once before and even escape from maximum security prison.

I cast my gaze downwards, studying the table in front of me. "Are we still safe?" I asked, my voice barely above a whisper. "Can they get in?"

He placed a gentle hand under my chin, lifting my head so that I met his gaze. "We have some of the best security money can buy," he reassured me. "No one can get in here without our authorization. They so much as touch that gate or fence, and it will kill them instantly." His words were firm, and I could sense the conviction behind them, making me feel somewhat safer and more secure.

Caught in his intense gaze, I took a deep breath to steady myself. He released my chin, but immediately took hold of my arm, urging me closer with a firm pressure. "Come here, baby girl," he commanded, pulling me towards him.

I rose from my seat and allowed him to guide me until I was straddling his lap, facing him. He then wrapped my arms around his neck before enveloping me in his own embrace, his strong arms encircling my waist.

We remained in each other's embrace for a few moments longer, holding onto the comfort that our closeness provided. His forehead was still pressed against mine, his breath was a warm caress on my skin. Breaking the silence, he spoke softly, "I know you're scared."

With worry etched on my face, I shook my head slightly and admitted, "I'm not scared of him hurting me, Rome. I'm scared of him hurting any of you," my voice was heavy with emotion.

A faint smile appeared on his lips, and he pulled me even closer, holding me tightly. "You're worried for us, baby girl?" he asked with a hint of amusement in his voice.

I reached up and gripped his hair gently, feeling the soft strands between my fingers. "Don't laugh at me," I pleaded.

Rome's gaze became intense and serious as he looked into my eyes, his voice was firm and unwavering. "Listen to me, Lexi," he commanded. "I know things have been moving fast between us, but never doubt for a moment how quickly we would stand between you and anything that tries to harm you." His words were filled with conviction, and he continued to stare at me, conveying his absolute belief in what he was saying.

"Do you understand?" He asked, seeking affirmation.

I nodded, but he shook his head at me, his expression unyielding. "Words, remember, Lexi," he commanded.

"Yes, Rome. I understand," I replied, my voice barely above a whisper.

He flashed a grin and effortlessly lifted me out of his lap, his hand landing with a playful smack on my ass. I stumbled slightly, my face flushing with heat.

"Good, now go relax with a movie while I finish what I'm working on. It's Hunt's turn to cook dinner tonight," he said, his eyes alight with amusement.

I couldn't help but wonder why they all seemed to enjoy smacking my ass.

Chapter 32

Alexis

Rome soon abandoned his laptop on the dining table and strolled over to the couch to join me. As soon as he settled in next to me, my attention shifted away from the movie that was playing. I turned to face him and leaned against the arm of the couch. Rome mirrored my actions, realizing that I was focused on him instead of the screen. After a moment, he lifted his knee against the back of the couch and cradled my feet in his lap, rubbing his fingers along the arches, eliciting a contented hum and sigh from me as I settled more comfortably into my seat.

With a raised eyebrow, I addressed him, "So..."

A small smile tugged at the corner of Rome's lips as he glanced down at my feet and then back up to my face. "So..." he echoed.

I took a moment to think about how I wanted to word my question before I asked, "So how did you come to like what you like?"

He chuckled quietly and looked at me again. "Are we talking about my movie choices? Or computers and hacking? Or are we talking about food again?" He said with laughter still in his voice.

I snorted at him and wiggled my toes in his hands. "No, we're taking about fucking."

He hummed at me, still pressing his thumbs into the arch of my foot.

"Were you like Christian Grey, did you have your own Mrs Robinson?" I asked.

He barked out a laugh, his voice echoing around the room.

"No, I didn't have a Mrs. Robinson. And I was definitely an adult before I got into the lifestyle." He replied before looking out one of the windows and I could see he was trying to decide how to tell me something.

I patiently waited for him to speak. I knew they all had things in their past that made them who they were. I couldn't deny that what I had gone through hadn't shaped who I now was as a person.

"My past wasn't a pleasant one. I know we can all say that to some degree but I can't recall a single pleasant memory from my childhood. We moved a lot when I was growing up and it wasn't until I was a lot older that I realized it was so they couldn't connect all the medical records." His voice is devoid of emotion.

I could sense the weight of his words and the pain that he carried with him. I didn't want to interrupt him, so I just listened intently as he continued to speak.

"My mother was diagnosed with a mental illness when I was very young. It was a very difficult situation for my family, and my father struggled to keep things together. He was physically abusive towards my mother and me, and I witnessed a lot of terrible things growing up. I became very withdrawn and isolated, and I found it difficult to connect with people."

He took a momentary pause before speaking, and I could see the visible anguish etched onto his face. It was clear that discussing his past was a challenging task for him and it made my heart ache for the boy he was. And for the man he was now.

"I eventually left home on the day of my seventeenth birthday and joined the military. It provided me with an escape from my past and a chance to start anew. I had always been adept with computers; they were my way of escaping mentally since I couldn't physically escape my reality. The military only enhanced my skills further."

He let out a deep breath before continuing, "Computers allowed me to be in control, to control anything and everything from behind a screen. I could monitor and keep a watchful eye on anyone I wanted to. I could manipulate schedules to my advantage. And when I was in control, my world felt more balanced. It allowed for moments of peace and even occasional bouts of happiness."

I could see the strength in his eyes as he spoke. Despite everything he had been through, he had managed to come out the other side.

"I won't deny that I started having sex early, and it's not like I didn't or don't enjoy sex without the other elements. It was pure coincidence that I stumbled across a club when I was on military leave once, I had no friends yet at that time and of course I was never going to ever return home again so I traveled and tried to experience everything I could."

A smile played on his lips as he reminisced about the memories, and I found myself wishing I could have witnessed that version of him.

"It was a very eye opening experience. I had read about places like that, I mean who hasn't, but to see it right in front of me was totally different. There was a guy there that started talking to me that very first night. He was a Dom and he could see I was very new to it, so he took me under his proverbial wing so to speak. He showed me what it was like to play with a submissive, and the feeling you get when they give you complete control over them. I never once looked back from that moment on."

"I'm sorry for what you had to go through," I said finally, not knowing what else to say.

"It's okay," he replied with a small smile. "It's made me who I am today, and I'm okay with that. I am who I am. I know some women can't cope with this side of me, it means a lot that you can."

"So what about the Dom, are you still friends?" I asked, sticking with the safer subject.

He gave a half laugh. "Yes we are, he actually connected me with Colt also as he knew him and knew we could connect on the military side of my life."

I tilted my head confused. "How does Colt know him? Colt said he didn't have the same kink for being called 'Sir.'" A smile tugged at my lip at the recollection.

Rome let out another laugh, and it was a relief to hear a lighter note after the solemn conversation we just had. "I'll need you to recount that conversation to me, but no, they didn't meet each other at the club. He was Colt's foster brother."

I was stunned silent having finally learnt a small detail of Colt's past. It was a small but significant detail that added another layer to the mysterious man that was Colt. While I collected my thoughts, Rome put my foot back down on the ground and leaned forward, bracing his hands on the arm of the couch on either side of me. He softly brushed his lips against mine before pulling back again. I felt a jolt of electricity run through my body at the touch of his lips. It was a soft and gentle kiss, but it sent my heart racing.

He leaned in closer, his breath hot against my lips as he spoke softly. "Can I tell you something else?" he whispered.

"Of course," I replied, feeling a flutter of excitement in my chest at the intimacy of the moment.

"I was worried," he began hesitantly, "that you wouldn't be able to accept that part of me. That you wouldn't be okay with my need for control like that in the bedroom."

I looked into his eyes, seeing the vulnerability and insecurity there. It was a side of him I hadn't seen before, and it made me feel closer to him. "I understand," I said gently, placing a hand on his cheek. "But you don't have to worry. I accept all of you, including that part of you."

Relief flooded his features, and he leaned in to kiss me deeply. As we broke apart, he smiled at me gratefully. "Thank you," he whispered.

A smile tugged at my lips. "You don't need to thank me."

He let out a contented hum and placed a gentle kiss on my lips once more before standing up from the couch and offering his hand to me. "Looks like it's time for dinner. Let's go, baby girl," he said, his tone affectionate as he pulled me up from the couch.

Chapter 33

Alexis

The following afternoon, I had just finished a refreshing shower and was making my way towards the stairs that led down to the lounge room when I saw Gabe. He appeared at the top of the stairs with a mischievous grin, coming up from downstairs. His presence immediately brought a smile to my face, and I paused, waiting for him to get closer.

"Hey," I said softly in greeting as he approached me with a confident stride.

"Hey, beautiful," he replied in a low and intimate voice, his eyes fixed on me. Suddenly, he slid a hand around the back of my neck, and his fingers entwined themselves in my hair, tugging me closer to him. As his lips pressed to mine, a shiver ran down my spine, and I felt myself melt into his arms.

Between kisses, I murmured, "I thought you would be sparing with Colt."

Gabe made a humming sound, the vibration of it moving through my entire body, and continued to feather kisses against my lips. "He's on a call, so I figured I would seek other forms of exercise."

I could feel Gabe's lips form a smile against mine as I started to giggle, but before I could fully break away, he sealed his mouth against mine, deepening the kiss and starting a fire in me. His tongue slid into my mouth, tangling with mine, and I felt his hand gripping my hip with an intensity that sent a pulse of heat straight through me.

As the intensity of the kiss heightened, my body responded with fervor, and I was lost in the sensation. The fire inside me grew stronger, and I wrapped my arms tightly around his neck, pulling him closer, and he responded by deepening the kiss. His hand tightened around my hair, sending tiny sparks of pain through me from where his fingers were gripping, and I let out a moan of pure ecstasy, unable to resist the pleasure.

We began to move backward, and I stumbled slightly, but his strong hands kept me steady, guiding me effortlessly. Although I was momentarily confused about where we were going, my mind was consumed by the feel of his lips on mine, and I trusted him to lead us where we needed to go.

At that moment, I was not aware of anything else but the sensations of his body pressed against mine, the taste of his kiss, and the feel of his hands on me. Every movement he made was met with a response from my body, and I followed his lead without hesitation, lost in the intensity of the moment.

I noticed that he bypassed my room and a few others before we finally came to a stop. His hand left my hip, and I heard the distinct sound of a door opening behind me. A thrill of excitement coursed through me as I realized he had brought me to his room.

Suddenly, the door slammed shut behind us and I was pressed against it with a force that took my breath away. Gabe's hand slid down my leg, gripping it tightly as he lifted it around his hip. The movement allowed him to grind his hard cock into my pussy, sending shivers of desire down my spine. I let out a groan of pleasure as my lips parted from his and my head fell back against the door. Gabe took advantage of the position, kissing and nipping down my throat with fervor.

"I've been hard since I listened to you cum yesterday." His words against my skin sent a rush of heat straight to my core.

I couldn't resist the urge to move against him, my hips rocked forward to grind myself against his hard length. He responded with a deep, guttural moan as he bit down on the flesh at the top of my breast. His tongue dragged up my throat before thrusting back into my mouth, his hips thrust against mine at the same time. The force of his movements pressed my hips into the wood of the door, causing a delicious pain that only made me wetter.

He yanked at the material of the shirt I had put on after my shower before he pulled away from my lips to pant, "Take this off before I fucking tear it from your body." The urgency in his voice sent a jolt of arousal through me, and I quickly complied, eager to feel his hands and mouth on my bare skin. My fingers fumbled with the hem of the shirt, tugging it up and over my head, revealing my bare breasts to him. A guttural groan escaped his lips as he took in the sight before him.

He released my leg and stepped back, his gaze fixed on my exposed flesh. In one swift movement, he bent down and took one of my nipples into his mouth, teasing it with the metal piercing in his tongue. My head fell back against the door with a moan as he bit down on the hard tip, sending a bolt of electricity through my body.

Desperate to feel his skin against mine, I started pulling at his shirt, struggling to get it off. As he released my nipple, I took hold of the fabric and pulled it over his head. With the shirt discarded, I quickly stripped off my leggings, feeling my body tremble with anticipation.

As he reached for his track pants to push them down, I dropped to my knees in front of him, eager to feel him in my mouth. I gripped his hard cock in my hand, before I slid my tongue from his balls to his tip, savoring the taste and feel of him. Without hesitation, I swallowed him down, taking him as deep as I could with a moan.

"Jesus, fuck!" he shouted, his low groan echoing through the room as he buried his hand in my hair. I hollowed my cheeks and began to move my mouth along his cock, opening my throat to take him even deeper. His grip on my hair tightened painfully, causing me to moan around him while he was buried in my throat. Another deep groan escaped him before he pulled me back off his cock, dragging me up his body until he could wrap his hand around my throat and hold me in place as his mouth crashed back into mine. The sensation of his lips on mine, combined with the pressure of his hand around my throat, sent a shiver of excitement down my spine.

He released both of his hands, and the sudden rush of cool air sent shivers down my spine. Then, he grabbed my waist and lifted me effortlessly, walking us across the room until he tossed me onto the bed. I gasped as I landed on the soft mattress, and before I could even collect myself, he was on top of me, his mouth crashing into mine with a fierce intensity. Our tongues tangled together in a heated dance that left me breathless and wanting more.

But I didn't just want to be a passive participant this time. With a surge of confidence, I wrapped a leg around his hip and used my weight to roll him under me until I was straddling his waist. His hard cock was trapped between our bodies, and I could feel it twitching with need. I took his wrists and moved them to hold them against the mattress on either side of his head, asserting my dominance.

He looked up at me with dark, hungry eyes, and his voice was low and husky as he spoke. "You're so fucking hot when you do that, beautiful." He thrust his hips upward, pressing his hard cock against me as if to prove a point.

I let out a deep, guttural moan as I ground down against him. "Do what?" I asked, my voice thick with desire.

He leaned up to lick his tongue against my panting mouth, his piercing brushing against my lips. "When you let me peek at the total badass you are," he whispered, his words sent shivers down my spine.

I could feel the heat rising between us, and I couldn't resist smashing my mouth against his again, my lips and tongue dancing with his in a fiery embrace.

He pulled his wrists from my grasp and sat up, his hands and momentum sent me on to my back again with a thud. He used his hands to roll and lift my body until my ass was in the air before him, then gently spread my legs and ass cheeks apart. With his tongue, he traced a path from my clit all the way to my entrance, and I couldn't help but moan with pleasure. I was grateful that my face was buried in the blanket, muffling the sound of my voice, or the whole house would know what we were up to.

He pushed his tongue inside me, then moved it back down to circle and flick against my clit. The sensation of his piercing against it was almost too much to bear, and I was rapidly approaching the point of no return. "Oh, fuck," I moaned, my voice muffled by the blanket. He continued to lick and suck at my clit, bringing me closer and closer to the brink of ecstasy.

"You close, beautiful?" he murmured against my sensitive flesh.

"God, yes, please," I begged, my body trembling. I didn't even know exactly what I was begging for, but I was aching and on the edge of cumming.

I let out a frustrated whimper as Gabe removed his mouth from my pussy, leaving me craving more. Then his beautiful cock was there, he slid it through the wetness he had previously left behind, coating himself before positioning the head at my entrance. And then, with one swift thrust, he slammed all the way home, dragging a muffled scream from me.

As he leaned over me, he grabbed a handful of my hair, pulling my face away from the blankets so he could whisper into my ear. "When you cum, it's going to be on my cock," he promised, sending a shiver down my spine.

Using his other hand to grip my hip, he pulled back almost fully before thrusting back into me with force, causing our hips to slap together solidly. The intense sensation propelled me over the edge and I cried out as my body shattered around him, pulsing and squeezing his cock as an orgasm ripped through me.

"That's it, beautiful, squeeze my cock," he moaned, urging me on. He pulled out and thrust back into me in shallow, hard movements, his skin slapped against mine with each thrust.

After letting me ride out my orgasm, he tightened the grip of both his hands, using them to hold me still as he dragged his cock back out of me inch by inch before slamming it home again. The sound of our skin slapping against each other filled the room as he continued to pound into me, his thrusts grew faster and harder, driving me to the brink of yet another orgasm. As the tension built in my body, I could feel my pussy start to clench around him with each of his movements. But then, to my surprise, he slowed down almost to a stop.

"Are you staying or going?" he asked, catching me off guard.

Confused, I started to say something about the randomness of his question, but then Gabe used his grip on my hair to pull my head up even further. My mouth fell open in a pant as I caught sight of Hunt frozen in the doorway. It's clear that he had just come back from a workout.

"Not that I don't appreciate this view of Lexi," Hunt breathed out, sounding both amused and exasperated as his eyes ran hotly over my naked body. "But was there a reason you chose my bed?"

Chapter 34

Alexis

Oh my fucking god, as Gabe dragged me into the room, I had assumed it was his own, but now I realize that he had planned this all along. I couldn't help but curse him silently under my breath. The asshole did this on purpose.

The asshole in question chose that moment to pull his cock almost all the way out of my pussy again before thrusting back in hard and making my moan echo around the room.

Hunt quickly moved into the room and shut the door behind him. He leaned back against it as he took in the view of us on his own fucking bed.

"Fuck, you look stunning like that, sweetheart," he growled, his voice thick with desire as he drank in the sight of my heaving chest and flushed skin.

As Hunt's eyes continued to roam over my curves, I couldn't help but notice the unmistakable bulge in his gym pants. His cock was already hard, tenting the fabric and begging to be freed.

As Gabe thrust into me again, the sound of our flesh slapped together and echoed throughout the room, making me moan uncontrollably.

Hunt stalked towards me with predatory intent, his eyes locked on mine. "Where do you want my cock, sweetheart?" His voice was laced with lust, making my stomach clench with need.

For a moment, I was confused, until Gabe's thumb slid against my rear entrance, pressing firmly and sending a jolt of pleasure through my body. I gasped and arched my back, pushing my hips towards him, eagerly begging for more. Hearing my pleasure, Hunt's eyes narrowed with understanding at what Gabe had done. He took a step closer toward me, his voice was low and dangerous as he asked, "Has anyone been there, sweetheart?"

Moaning again at the sensation of Gabe's thumb pressing harder against me, I was unable to form words to respond, instead I nodded my head as my body begged for more.

At my response Gabe swiftly removed his hand from my ass and leaned over me. He wrapped his hand around the front of my throat, bending me further up towards him as he bit my ear in a sharp nip.

"I don't think you realize that the thought of you with anyone but us makes me want to burn the world down," he growled, his voice was thick with desire. The intensity of his words made my stomach clench and my pussy tightened around his cock.

He groaned as he felt my reaction, his hand tightened around my throat, which only heightened my arousal. "Do you like when we talk like that, beautiful?" he moaned in my ear, giving a shallow thrust. "Do you like hearing us tell you we will kill anyone who touches you?"

Fuck. Me.

My eyes rolled back in my head as I moaned loudly, the sound echoed around the room. I could feel the tension building in my body, and I knew I was close to the edge.

As he nipped at my ear once more, I felt his hot breath on the side of my face, sending shivers down my spine. "You are ours," he growled.

He thrust into me again as his hand squeezed possessively on my throat and I panted for him.

He leaned in closer, his lips brushing against my earlobe as he continued to speak in a low, gravelly voice. "You belong to us, and only us. No one else can touch you like this, make you feel like this."

As he thrust into me again, my body shuddered with pleasure and I moaned loudly. His words sent shockwaves of desire through me, and I felt myself getting wetter with every passing second.

"We don't have supplies here to take you together so my brother will just have to cope with you choking on his cock," he growled into my ear. "But once we are out of here, beautiful, I'm going to fuck your gorgeous ass while you ride him. And then we are going to cum all over your hot and spent body until there is no mistaking that you're ours."

His words were like a punch to my gut, making my head spin with desire. I could feel my orgasm building again, the raspy words dripping from his mouth were almost enough to make me cum right then and there. I let out a soft moan as he released his grip on my throat and I dropped forward onto my hands, gasping for breath, right in front of Hunt's bare cock.

Hunt took hold of my chin, his thumb tracing over my bottom lip as he bent down to look into my face. "Hey, sweetheart. You good?" he asked, his voice filled with tenderness.

Gabe chose that moment to dig his hands into my hips and thrust into me again, causing me to arch my back and cry out. "God, yes!" I moaned, my body on fire with pleasure.

Hunt snickered at my response, his eyes flicked behind me to his brother before he looked at me again. He moved forward, capturing my moans in a deep, passionate kiss. His mouth and tongue worked hard against mine, leaving me breathless and wanting more.

He pulled away from the kiss and slid both of his hands into my hair, gathering it all together at the back of my head in a tight hold. "Open that gorgeous mouth, sweetheart," he commanded, his voice filled with desire. "I want to see those beautiful lips wrapped around my cock."

I obeyed without hesitation, letting my mouth fall open as he slid his hard length into my waiting mouth. I pressed my tongue against the underside of him all the way in, causing Hunt to elicit a deep groan that vibrated through his whole body.

He gave a few tentative thrusts in and out of my mouth, moaning in pleasure. "Fuck, you feel so good," he rasped. He slowly pushed further into my mouth, bumping the back of my throat. "Can I fuck your throat, sweetheart?"

With my mouth still full of him, I nodded eagerly, knowing that's exactly what he wanted. Just then, Gabe thrust into me hard, pushing me further onto Hunt's cock, forcing it down my throat.

I moaned around Hunt, my body shaking with pleasure.

"Fuck!" Hunt cried out as he pulled completely out of my mouth, panting heavily. I heard Gabe snicker behind me, his hands still firmly gripping my hips. Hunt growled, a deep and primal sound that sent shivers down my spine

With a tight hold on my hair, Hunt tapped the head of his cock against my lips, silently commanding me to open my mouth again. I complied eagerly, and he thrust all the way in again until his entire length was buried in my throat. My nose brushed against his pelvis, and I swallowed around the head of him, eliciting a loud and obscene groan from him.

He pulled back and thrust into my throat again, holding himself there briefly before withdrawing once more. The next time he withdrew, Gabe took advantage, thrusting into me hard and pushing me onto Hunt's cock as he began to push in again. The combination of their movements created an intense sensation that made me moan around Hunt's cock once more.

Their pace quickened, and I could feel myself on the brink of orgasm. Hunt's hand tightened in my hair as he continued to thrust into my throat, his groans growing louder with each passing moment. Gabe's hands gripped my hips tightly as he thrust into me, sending waves of pleasure coursing through my body. The sound of his skin slapping against mine echoed around the room.

"Fuck, this mouth feels so fucking good." Hunt gritted out.

I was moaning uncontrollably now, loud enough to make a porn star proud, my body writhing with pleasure as they took me in tandem. It's as if they were reading my mind, knowing exactly what I needed and giving it to me with expert precision. I was lost in the sensation, lost in the pleasure, lost in them.

Gabe's hand found its way to my clit, and as he started rubbing it in tight circles, I could feel myself climbing higher and higher towards an intense orgasm.

My moans were becoming louder and more urgent as Hunt relentlessly thrust his cock into my mouth, his movements became more forceful with each stroke, his cock pushing deeper and deeper down my throat. Meanwhile, Gabe's fingers worked their magic on my clit, igniting waves of pleasure throughout my body. My limbs trembled as I teetered on the brink of orgasm, the sensation built to an almost unbearable level

"I'm going to cum," Hunt gasped out and his movements began to falter and his rhythm started to stutter.

Gabe stopped moving, his hand withdrawing from my clit, and my orgasm slid away. But then, Gabe leaned over my body again, his hand wrapping around my throat as he whispered in my ear. His voice was low and raspy, urging me on. "That's it, beautiful," he said, "swallow all of his cum and I'll let you finish." And then, he tightened his grip on my throat, forcing it to close around the head of Hunt's cock.

With a final, guttural curse, Hunt's body convulsed as he exploded, his cum shooting down my throat with a forceful groan. I obediently swallowed every drop, feeling the warm liquid slide down my throat. Hunt pulled out and staggered back, collapsing into the armchair in the corner of the room, spent and breathless.

Gabe used the grip he had around my neck to lift my upper body almost to an upright position, arching my back painfully, before he withdrew his cock almost entirely and thrust back inside me with a force that sent a sharp slapping sound echoing through the room. My body is instantly propelled back towards the brink of orgasm. He repeated the motion and I let out a loud moan.

He then resumed a slow, powerful rhythm, pulling out inch by inch and then slamming back into me. I can feel my pussy clenching around him, my orgasm tantalizingly close but just out of reach. His voice growled into my ear, "You're such a good fucking girl. Are you going to cum on my cock again, beautiful? You're squeezing it so fucking hard you're going to make me cum too. Do you want my cum?"

I reached around his head and grabbed a fistful of his hair and whispered hoarsely, "Don't just talk about it, do it. Give me your cum. I want it deep inside me."

He groaned in response. "Fuck, that's so fucking hot." His pace quickened once again, his body slamming into mine with increasing intensity. His other hand traveled down my body and his fingers found my clit, circling it slowly as he continued to thrust into me.

"Cum for me, beautiful. Cum all over my cock," he growled, before delivering a hard slap to my clit. My orgasm exploded through me, and I screamed as Gabe pounded into me with a jagged, uneven pace. He cursed and let out a low moan as he exploded deep inside me.

We collapsed on the bed in a sweaty heap, limbs entangled as we panted heavily in the now-silent room, trying to regain our composure.

Hunt's voice broke the silence as he said to his brother, "So, can we revisit the question of why you chose my room?"

Chapter 35

Hunt

Gabe chuckled, his chest still heaving from the intensity of our recent activities. "I thought it would be more fun," he teased, earning a groan from me.

I rolled my eyes, but there was a smile tugging at the corner of my mouth. "Well, I hope you got your fill of fun," I quipped.

Gabe laughed and leaned over to give Lexi a lazy kiss on the lips before rolling onto his back, his arm draped over his eyes. "Oh, I definitely did," he said.

I heaved myself out of the armchair and slowly stalked towards the bed. I could see Lexi's eyes following my movements, looking over my whole body as I made my way towards her.

I ignored Gabe completely though my words were for him. "Well then you can continue your own fun in your own shower." I said as I then bent and lifted Lexi out of the bed and curled her against me with an arm under her back and her legs.

With a giggle, Lexi wrapped an arm around my neck and waved her fingers towards Gabe, her gaze flickering between the two of us. My heart beat faster at the sight of her, her tousled hair and flushed cheeks made her look more beautiful than ever.

I carried her towards the bathroom, ignoring Gabe's grumbling as we made our way through the door. As I stepped into the shower, I set Lexi down gently and turned on the water, adjusting the temperature until it was just right.

As the water cascaded over us, Lexi leaned back against me, her body fitting perfectly against mine. I wrapped my arms around her, holding her close as we let the warmth wash over us.

I had thought telling her about my past might have changed the way she saw me, that she might think negatively about me, but if anything it just brought her closer to me.

Under the stream of water, I closed my eyes and let out a contented sigh. Having Lexi in my arms like this feels like home, like everything was right with the world. I never knew I could feel this way about someone, but with Lexi, it was different. She accepted me for who I was, flaws and all, and that was a feeling I had never experienced before.

I wasn't sure what the others felt towards Lexi, but I knew I didn't want this to end when Dominick was captured again. I didn't want to let go of this feeling that was digging its way into my heart.

Feeling the need to express how I felt physically, I turned her around to face me and guided us towards the shower wall, pressing my body against hers. I kissed her gently, savoring the feeling of her lips against mine, before my hands explored her curves, finding the weight of her breasts and giving them a gentle squeeze. Her moans of pleasure fueled my desire as I deepened the kiss and slowly made my way down her body, kneeling on the shower floor to worship her on my knees.

I reached for the movable shower head and turned the water on to that also, causing her to ask in a breathless voice what I was doing. I gently washed her pussy with the water and a little soap before running it along her legs, from her thigh to her toes and back up again. Her moans of pleasure drove me wild with desire, but I remained focused on pleasuring her.

I repeated the process on her other leg before lifting it and hooking it over my shoulder. I directed the water spray over her pussy once more, causing her to moan even louder. With a deep breath, I slid my tongue through her wet folds, circling her clit and then back down to her entrance. Her hand tightened painfully in my hair as I continued to explore her with my tongue, her hips ground against my mouth. I trailed my fingers along her entrance, sliding them in and out of her while I continued to lick and suck on her clit while the water from the shower head massaged where my mouth moved over her.

I directed the showerhead away briefly to give her reprieve and to allow me to draw in a breath before bringing it even closer and directing it straight onto her clit as I flick my tongue back and forth over it. She moaned loudly and tightened hard around my fingers as they moved inside her.

She was so responsive to my touch, and it was driving me crazy with desire. Being surrounded by the sweet noises she made along with the sounds of the shower and nothing else made that moment with her even more erotic.

I hooked my fingers inside her, rubbing over her G-spot as I sucked her clit into my mouth. She shattered, her body pulsing and clenching around my fingers as she cums. When she whimpered, I gentled my mouth to soft dragging licks and I hung the shower head back up on its hook. I was still moving my fingers softly in and out of her as I used my other hand to lift the leg that was over my shoulder, holding it up and outward as I dragged my body back up to standing.

Her head had fallen back against the shower wall with her eyes closed and her breathing was ragged.

I pulled my fingers slowly from inside her and used that same hand to guide my cock to push slowly into her pussy. Her eyes widened at me, I'm sure she was over sensitive from already taking Gabe but I needed to be close to her.

I moved slowly, savoring every sensation as I slid deeper into her. Her body was so warm and welcoming, and I could feel her inner muscles clenching around me as I moved. There were no sounds apart from the shower and our moans making the moment beyond intimate.

I lifted her other leg and she wrapped both of her legs around my waist, pulling me in closer as we moved together. Our bodies were slick with water and sweat, and I could feel my own desire building with each slow drag of my cock inside her. I buried my face in her neck, breathing in her scent as I continued to move slowly in and out of her.

Her moans were growing louder now, and I knew that she was close to the edge. I reached down between us, finding her clit and softly brushing over it with my thumb.

She arched her back, pressing her body harder against mine as I continued to stroke her clit. I could feel her walls tightening around me, and I knew she was about to cum again. I quickened my pace slightly, pushing deeper into her as she moaned my name.

With a final low moan, she tensed and pulsed around me, her orgasm washing over her in waves and dragging me over the cliff after her until I was cumming deep inside her.

We stood there for a moment, panting and clinging to each other as the water from the shower continued to rain down on us. I held her close, still buried inside her as we caught our breath. I kissed her gently on the lips, savoring the taste of her. When I finally pulled out of her and set her back down on her feet I wrapped my hands around the sides of her neck and used my thumbs to direct her face up to mine as I went back to brushing my lips across hers softly.

I stopped kissing her with a soft sigh and rested my forehead against hers for a few moments before I went back to slowly washing her beautiful body. Once I was done I did a quick wash of my own as she relaxed back against the shower wall under part of the spray of water.

Moving back over to her, I slid my hands gently along her face, brushing her wet strands away as she looked at me with an affection I never hoped to see directed towards me.

"Lexi, I-" My confession was cut off with her fingers against my lips as she shook her head softly.

She whispered to me, "Let's discuss it tomorrow," and then leaned in to give me a soft kiss before leaving the shower. I turned off the water and followed her out, grabbing a large fluffy towel from the rack. I took my time drying her and then myself before we made our way back to the bed.

Gabe was already there with a set of comfortable clothes for Lexi from her room, while I headed to my closet to grab something for myself. After changing I left the closet light on for her and we crawled under the covers together. Lexi snuggled up against me, with Gabe curled up around her back, and we all laid there in silence.

I ran my fingers through her hair, savoring the feel of the soft strands between my fingers. Eventually, we drifted off to sleep, wrapped up in each other's embrace.

Chapter 36

Alexis

For once I woke with the sun, the sky outside had not long started to light up with the first rays of sunlight. The twins had still disappeared before me but not by much, the sheets still toasty on either side of me.

After showering again in my own room, I dressed quickly and made my way towards the stairs to head down for breakfast. As I walked, I saw Sam appear at the top of the stairs, making her way towards me. Despite always forgetting when she was supposed to arrive, I could tell that she was earlier than usual today.

"Hey Sam, you're really early, trying to get ahead of the day?" I asked, smiling at her.

"I'm so sorry, Alexis," she replied, the miserable look she gave me told me everything I needed to know. "They have Nathan."

I saw the needle in her hand seconds before she tried to stab it into my neck. I reacted quickly, my hand shooting out to knock the needle away from her grip. It clattered across the floor, just out of her reach. We both scrambled for it, but

I managed to land on top of her, pinning her to the ground, causing her to turn and try to push me off. She fought back, scratching and clawing at my skin, drawing blood with a deep slice to the side of my throat with her sharp nails.

I recoiled in pain and pressed my hand to the wound, hoping to staunch the bleeding. In that moment of distraction, Sam lunged for the needle again. But I was not going down without a fight. I grabbed a fistful of her hair and yanked her backwards, eliciting a scream from her lips. I held on tight, pulling until I could feel the strands of hair tearing away from her scalp.

Before I could do anything else, an explosion rocked the room, shaking the walls and causing debris to rain down from the ceiling. Sam's crying intensified, but I was too preoccupied to pay attention to her now. "What the fuck did you do?" I shouted at her, my heart racing with fear and adrenaline.

She could only cry harder in response. It's clear that she wouldn't be giving me any answers, so I took matters into my own hands. I pulled out my gun from where it was hidden and struck her hard with the butt of the weapon. Sam's body crumpled to the ground, completely unconscious.

Quickly releasing her, I scrambled over and snatched up the needle, examining it closely. Hoping against hope that it was just a sedative, since I doubted Dominick would let anyone but himself kill me, I pressed the sharp point into Sam's skin and plunged the plunger down, forcing the liquid into her bloodstream.

"Colt!" I screamed, the sound of my voice echoing through the empty halls. But before I could even finish calling his name, he appeared from the direction of the stairs, running towards me with a sense of urgency. His eyes widened as he saw the motionless figure lying at my feet, and without hesitation, he grabbed my hand and pulled me into the nearest bedroom.

"Grab a vest," he commanded, pointing towards the side of the bed where I knew they kept at least one stored. Meanwhile, he darted towards the closet, swiftly returning with a handful of guns. He turned me around and shoved another firearm into the back of my pants, his movements quick and calculated.

At that very moment, the house shook with a deafening explosion, the ground beneath our feet trembling with each passing second. "Follow me closely," he instructed, his voice low and tense. "We need to get you out of here."

Without a moment's hesitation, I nodded in agreement and followed him closely as we made our way back out into the hallway. I could feel the weight of the gun in my hand. Colt led the way, his own gun at the ready, scanning the hallway for any signs of movement.

As we reached the top of the stairs, a shadowy figure appeared out of nowhere, dressed in full black tactical clothing. In a sudden burst of motion, the attacker knocked Colt's gun to the side and launched himself towards Colt.

Without a moment's hesitation, I raised my own gun, aiming with unwavering precision at the attacker's head and I pulled the trigger.

The impact of a body the size of a mountain colliding with my side caused my shot to go wide, my gun careened over the edge of the landing and clattered to the floor below.

I struggled and struck out at the massive body that was pressing against me, my fists and elbows lashed out with all the force I could muster. It quickly became apparent that I was hopelessly outmatched. Just as I was about to strike a well-aimed blow to the attacker's temple, another man suddenly appeared, grabbing both of my wrists with a strength that left me gasping in pain.

With a deftness that spoke of years of experience, the assailant secured zip tie restraints around my wrists, rendering me helpless and unable to defend myself. The man backhanded me with a brutal force that left me reeling, blood dripping from my split lip and onto the floor below. He moved with an agility that would have been impressive under any other circumstances, before using my tied wrists to hoist me up and over his shoulder like a lifeless sack of potatoes. My ankles were swiftly bound with more restraints, and we began to move towards the stairs.

"Lexi!" I heard Colt's desperate cry, my heart racing in response. I struggled to lift my head, the pain in my body making it difficult to move. Suddenly, Colt appeared, bloodied and bruised, charging towards us with a fierce determination in his eyes. But before I could even process the relief of his presence, the man next to me raised his gun and fired back at Colt with deadly accuracy.

Time seemed to slow down as I watched the bullet hit Colt's chest, sending him flying backwards over the landing. I heard the sickening crash of his body hitting the ground, the sound echoed through the house over the gunfire I could hear coming from various different directions.

A gut-wrenching scream escaped my lips as I witnessed the scene unfold before me.

As the mountain of a man ran down the stairs and through the ground level with me slung over his shoulder, I could see the body of Colt lying motionless on his side amidst the shattered debris of the dining table, his face covered in blood and his mouth hanging slack.

Panic gripped me as they carried me out of the house, and I was flung unceremoniously into the back of a dark van, the metal floor cold and hard beneath me. I could hear the urgent sound of footsteps running towards the van and a harsh voice from the front seat snapped, "We have sixty seconds to get out of here before it's all set to blow."

Despite my restraints, I screamed and thrashed my body, determined to fight back. The man restraining me grunted in pain as I managed to land a blow that must have hurt him.

"Shut her up!" he barked, and I barely had time to register his words before I felt a sharp, stinging sensation in my neck as a needle pierced my skin. A wave of agony spread through me, and I screamed in protest, my body convulsing with the intensity of my fury. Despite my efforts to break free, the man's grip remained unyielding as the drug coursed through my veins, and I felt myself starting to slip away into unconsciousness, the darkness slowly starting to eat at the edges of my vision.

As the world around me blurred and faded, I was aware of the van lurching forward, the vibrations of the road jolting my senses. Through the back window, I watched as the house exploded into a fiery inferno, the flames leapt skyward as debris flew in every direction. Then, I felt and saw nothing but darkness.

The shadows and dark always win out somewhere.

To be continued...

SHATTERED SAFETY

BOOK 2

UNBREAKABLE

Coming Soon!

Author's Note

I hope that you enjoyed the first book in the Shattered Safety duet and being introduced to Lexi and the guys.

Please don't gather your pitchforks and flaming torches after that cliffhanger. The second book should be released in the middle of 2023, so not too long of a wait for you to find out what happened.

First off, thank you to my husband and my mum for always supporting me and putting up with my random obsessive personality that gets me totally lost in my writing etc. I am hoping that you don't get to read this line considering the contents of the book but if you do read this please do not let me know so I don't die of mortification.

I want to also say a huge thanks to Ash and Diana for being my own personal cheer leaders and alpha readers, without you I'm not sure I would have pushed myself as hard as I did to get this finished.

And to Jessica from Book Dragon Designs for your amazing work and putting up with all the questions and extra requests I threw at you.

Thank you also to all my betas and to my ARC team, for helping a completely unknown author.

And lastly thank you to you, my readers, for picking up this book and taking a chance on a baby author out of all the amazing authors out there, I completely appreciate it and you.

xx

Maree Rose

About the Author

Maree is a baby author who although she has been writing most of her life, never thought she would ever get something published, which is now why she published this herself. She has always been an avid reader since a young age after roaming through book exchanges with her mum when she was just starting to read serious big girl books.

Maree lives on the East Coast of Australia with her wonderful husband, her son and her two gorgeous squishy british bulldogs.

When she is not writing she is working in a financial career (for something completely different to the creative side) or she is working on her photography (which is just as hot as her books).